I0652995

**PURE
SLUSH
BOOKS**

praise for *Many Fish to Fry*

Enchanting is this novel set in Delhi, narrated by the quick-witted Reena, a housewife and mother who betters herself in middle-age by becoming a jewelry designer / entrepreneur, as well as the 'ear' for an eccentric Indian Private Eye who charms her with his energies and unrivalled intuition. Reena's life and the people around her evolve in ways she never imagined.

Many Fish to Fry has a great understated humor that doesn't flag, and held me tightly, clutching my cup of tea to its satisfying conclusion. A beautiful and very human story.

~ Susan Tepper, author of *The Merrill Diaries*

Many slices of life fried to a perfect crisp! Abha Iyengar's unmistakable eye for detail and the absurd makes for a quirky and layered novel. *Many Fish to Fry* is an intricate, well-paced and humorous look at marriages and lives around us.

~ Nandita Bose, author of *Tread Softly* and *The Perfume of Promise*

The many faces of the modern Indian woman: the victims and the survivors, the compromised and the entrepreneurial. A page-turner as rich as masala tea – the dhaba way.

~ Christopher Allen, author of *Conversations with S. Teri O'Type*

A cheerful tale with a distinct flavour of Delhi. Apartment intrigues, insecurities, the hunt for that perfectly cooked fish and endless cups of tea – a warm story that you can relate to!

~ Vasudev Murthy, author of *Sherlock Holmes in Japan*

Many Fish to Fry is about a woman happily squeezed between two generations – a woman *of* two generations...

Reena is starting her own business. She goes online for TED Talks. She supports her daughter's career, not only her son's. She is forever watching her weight. But Reena is also a woman who likes to stop a while for tea and gossip, as women did when they had more time on their hands. She still cooks for the whole family, fully-grown children included. And she calls her husband "liberated" for having made a cup of tea.

Many Fish to Fry provides a shock of recognition for anybody who has grown up in tradition but winks at the new world, behind her mother's back!

~ Luisa Brenta, author of *The Company of Men*

also by Abha Iyengar

Yearnings (Serene Woods)

Shrayan (Blue Pumpkin)

Flash Bites (Authorspress)

Shrayan and *Flash Bites*
are also available
as eBooks on Amazon
and Smashwords

MANY FISH to FRY

Abha IYENGAR

a Pure Slush book

Many Fish to Fry published by Pure Slush, October 2014.

Pure Slush Books
4 Warburton Street
Magill SA 5072
Australia

Front cover photograph copyright © Alan Witikoski
http://fenodesign.blogspot.com.br/

ISBN: 978-1-925101-59-1

Find *Pure Slush* at http://pureslush.webs.com

Copies of all *Pure Slush* publications can be bought
at http://pureslush.webs.com/store.htm

All queries re *Pure Slush* can be made
via email to edpureslush@live.com.au

Versions of the following chapters were
previously published online on *Pure Slush*:

Discordant Notes (April 2013)
Try Sharing the Bananas (July 2013)
Part of *Wired and Stoned* as *Wise and With It* (May 2013)

Dedicated to my sister

Vibha Mishra,

married to an Odia man

who loves fish.

To you, Vibs!

He often expressed

A curious wish,

To be interchangeably

Man and fish;

To nibble the bait

Off the hook,

Said he,

And then slip away

Like a ghost

In the sea.

~ *Ennui* by Marianne Moore

Instinct is a marvelous thing.

It can neither be explained nor ignored.

~ from *The Mysterious Affair at Styles* by Agatha Christie

Contents

Foreword / 17

I

The Turning Point / 21

Discoloured Walls / 26

Coloured View / 29

A Tenacious Hold / 31

Discordant Notes / 34

Forging an Identity / 37

II

The Big Jump / 41

Tea, Termites and Fish / 45

A Good Beginning / 48

The Scales / 52

Scheming Gods / 55

III

The Coming of Harinmoy Banerjee / 61

Butterfly, Dog, SS / 64

The Green Monster / 69

The Exercycle / 74

Try Sharing the Bananas / 78

IV

Wired and Stoned / 83

The Greedy and the Innocent / 88

Family Matters / 91

You Get What You Will / 93

Where is Anirban? / 97

A Village called Chirulia / 102

V

The Return of Harinmoy / 107

A Case to Crack / 113

Expressways and Fartiquette / 118

The Bajaj Wedding Sangeet / 123

Triple Whammy Plus One / 128

VI

A Matter of Perspective / 137

Dish without Fish / 141

White Shoes with Brass Buckles / 145

Unforgettable Due to Formula / 149

Crowning Glory / 153

The Fish Arrives / 156

Glossary / 161

Thanks / 165

About the Author / 167

Foreword

In *Many Fish to Fry*, Abha Iyengar examines some of India's deeper social issues in a thoughtful, yet light-hearted, humorous way, and illustrates the struggle to rise above the constraints of tradition, patriarchy and old-fashioned beliefs.

Iyengar's combination of colloquial language and Western slang mirror real-life trends of language and culture in India. Her deft hand with dialogue and use of Indian English bring the characters to life so well that they almost jump off the page. These characters are three-dimensional and engaging, from Delhi housewife Reena, with her wry approach to dealing with what a woman is expected to do or be versus what she wants, to Super Sleuth Harinmoy, with his colourful outfits and odd figures of speech.

Iyengar's poetic yet economical use of language speaks to all five senses. I can feel the touch of a welcome breeze through a thin sari on an oppressively hot day, and visualise the scales of the *Hilsa* fish glinting in the morning sunshine; the warm scents of various spices seem to fill my nose with their presence; I want to bite into the glistening *laddoo* Reena finds in her kitchen, and sip her "masala tea, (made) the *dhaba* way."

Many Fish to Fry is a pleasure for the intellect and the senses.

Chris Galvin Nguyen writes and edits in Canada and Viet Nam.

I

◆ 1 ◆

The Turning Point

Reena felt the fingers press into her face. Anjali the beautician was at work again.

The facial was no longer an indulgence; it was a necessity. At her age, forty-nine, Reena needed the facials to keep her skin looking as youthful as possible.

As Anjali's fingers smoothed the cream over Reena's face and then moved her fingers to rub the cream gently into her skin, Reena closed her eyes, trying hard to unwind. Her restless mind prevented her from doing this. She could never bring herself to relax. When she did her yoga, the deep breathing meditation that *pranayam* required was the most difficult thing for her to do.

Her mind wandered and she wondered about Anjali, who worked with two to three clients or more per day. She travelled long distances to her clients' homes to attend to their beauty needs: waxing, threading, facial, manicure, pedicure, massage. They would also come over to her home early morning or late evening, if their need for a beauty treatment was urgent and rushed. She was booked every day and Reena had to make a booking with her several days in advance.

Anjali's fingers were hard despite the softness of the cream she was kneading into Reena's face. They were a worker's hands, the hands of a woman who washed clothes, did the dishes and cooked the meals for the family along with her work as a beautician.

Anjali worked hard at being upwardly mobile, bringing in the money to pay for the extra expenses like tuition for her daughter and her son's cricket training.

Reena sighed. Her life seemed comparatively empty. Her kids had kept her busy when they were young. They were grown up now. Though they were still living at home, they were working adults who were out in the morning and back late evening or night. They did not need looking after and told her not to fuss when she enquired after them.

"Do your thing, Mom," they often told her. "Now you are free to do all the things you wanted to, but were afraid to..." and they would laugh and hug her and walk away.

Anand, her husband, had his work as a project consultant to occupy him, but she had nothing. She was not a kitty-party type, dressing up and hobnobbing with other women discussing dishes, film stars and fashion. Nor could she sit in the sun like some others, cutting vegetables and gossiping with neighbours. She did not watch soap operas like many women did to fill in the vacant hours.

She wanted involvement of some kind and she could not figure out what it was. She was middle-aged, and could not think of joining any company by taking up a job. Whatever she did now to occupy herself, would have to be some work of her own.

"Madam, how are you feeling?" Anjali's voice cut into her thoughts.

"Okay, Anjali," she said, looking up into her face.

Reena noticed the pendant. Two entwined fish hung from a long silver chain around Anjali's neck. It was one of those cheap designer things, not very expensive. *The design is good but the execution poor*, thought Reena, staring at the swinging fish.

If I improve the detailing and use a different metal, Reena thought, *the pendant could be really beautiful.* She had been good at sketching and designing and had designed jewellery in college for her friends for a lark but had never followed it up.

In those days, 'designer' was not a label a girl wanted attached to her name: school-teacher or happily-married (preferably to some well-heeled and handsome guy like in the Mills and Boon romances) were more sought-after terms. Happily-married-school-teacher was considered a very suitable end to any woman's ambitions.

"Anjali, where did you get this pendant?" Reena asked.

"Oh, from a roadside shop in Paharganj... you like it?"

"Hmm, it's nice," said Reena. "If it was crafted better, it would have been beautiful."

"Yes, Madam, but what do you expect... it is not expensive."

"I used to design jewellery, you know, for friends."

Anjali slathered more cream onto her palms. "Ma'am, how wonderful! And now?"

"And now... what?"

"If you do it now, it will be more wonderful." She said it without a smile, her look was serious. She kneaded the cream into Reena's neck.

"Gently, Anjali," Reena said. "Don't have to crush my collarbone."

"Sorry, Madam, I hope I did not say anything wrong?"

"No, actually you have just set me thinking."

"And that is bad?"

"No." Reena smiled through the layers of cream. "It's good."

~

Reena waited patiently with eyes closed as Anjali steamed her face with a hot towel, removed a few blackheads, rubbed an ice cube to close the pores, and then applied a cucumber-based peel-off mask to tighten the skin.

After the facial was over, Reena heaved a sigh of relief. Her skin felt soft and smooth. Though she hated to sit patiently through the beauty treatment, the end result was worth it.

But there are strange turning points in one's life and she was experiencing one.

"Anjali, give me your pendant. I will pay you for it. I hope you don't mind..."

"No, Ma'am, what are you saying, I will give it to you just like that, it costs little..."

"No, Anjali, I will pay you. I need to do this. I will use the pendant to begin my business."

Anjali's eyes lit up. "Oh, Madam, that is wonderful."

Reena gave her hand a squeeze. The hand was rough, the fingers tough. But she felt a sudden kinship with this young woman who worked so hard to make ends meet and also find meaning in her life. It was an expression of self through occupation.

Reena would design jewellery and sell it. She suddenly realized that this was what she had wanted to do all along.

"Madam, here is the pendant." While Reena had been busy with her thoughts, Anjali had removed the pendant from its chain and now held it out to her.

"Thank you, Anjali." Reena brought the pendant to her forehead and then kissed it. "You do not know what you have done. You have given me a life."

"Okay," Anjali said, tears in her eyes. "Madam, it is so important isn't it? To have meaning…"

Reena nodded. Her brain was already abuzz with ideas. "Do you have the street address of the shop?"

"No, Ma'am, but I can take you there."

They made a date to meet on the weekend at Paharganj. Anjali would squeeze time out from her busy schedule to help Reena start her business.

Discoloured Walls

Anjali had brought Reena to the roadside shop in Paharganj. The young man, Sanjay Singh, sold jewellery made of cheap metal, some of the pieces plated to look like gold. There were transparent and coloured plastics of various shapes, cut like gemstones. The workmanship was good and the necklaces, earrings, and rings were worth the price.

"Who buys from you?" Reena asked.

"Teenagers and housewives do. They don't want to spend much but still wish to feel and look good."

Reena picked up a few pieces, and asked him questions regarding the suppliers and the costing. He smiled and shared the information.

He invited them to his home, just behind the shop, to share a cup of tea. "My wife, Neeru, will be happy to meet you," he said.

Discoloured, faded walls and a cracked, uneven cement floor was what Reena saw when she entered the home of Sanjay Singh. However, the couple of stools for seating and the small round centre table were neatly placed and clean. She passed the small kitchen and noticed how the kitchen utensils, though few, shone in the morning light. Obviously, they were house-proud.

Sanjay's wife, Neeru, was young and pretty. She met them with shy eyes and offered them tea in small, thick, white china cups. The tea was very sweet and dark and though Reena wanted to leave it after a few sips, she forced herself to drink it.

"May I come again to talk with you?" she asked. She had already told Sanjay of her intention to design jewellery as a business.

"I am willing to help you in whichever way I can," he said.

Neeru smiled at Reena and said, "He is very hard-working."

Anjali said, "That is the one thing that my husband and I also do. Hard work. We have only ourselves to fall back on."

~

The auto-rickshaw, which they had taken to return home, turned into the narrow lane leading to Anjali's apartment building. Anjali stepped off and waved Reena a quick goodbye. As Reena watched Anjali disappear down her lane, she thought, *It is a start. I have made a beginning.*

The auto-rickshaw turned back into the traffic. Reena thought of how Sanjay and Neeru lived a precarious existence in a crowded Delhi street, with love and hard work as sustenance.

Opening her front door with her key, she kicked off her heels, changed into a T-shirt and pajamas and set to work. She fetched some paper from her husband's study and sharpened a couple of pencils. Then she began sketching, her hands feverish, her brain charged with energy. She would not make herself a cup of tea till she had a first design down on paper.

Several sketches later, Reena looked at the clock. It was 5pm... now she would have her tea. She stood up and surveyed the scene. Scattered sheets of paper lay on the floor, the dining table on which she had been working, the chair next to the one on which she sat. A whirlwind had entered her dining room.

She removed her spectacles and gazed at the final rough sketch of the first pendant she had designed. It was circular, a labyrinth of silver wire. She would thread a very fine gold wire through this, and at random points, stud it with nine tiny gemstones.

Her mind was calm and relaxed. She had found her centre.

• 3 •

Coloured View

It was tough; she was suddenly involved in something new, and beginning from scratch.

Reena's husband, Anand, had first been indulgent, thinking it was a new hobby of hers. When her seriousness with her work began to interfere with her attention to the little details around him, things she had taken care of earlier because she had nothing else on her mind, he expressed his disapproval.

"You are getting too involved. Why do you need to do all this running around at your age?"

This was followed then with some direct talk. "I miss the hot *rotis* you make for me. You seem to have no time to talk to me... and the *dhobi* just can't iron the shirts like you do... did. All you do is think design, do design, oh, I am sick of it!"

She had expected him to be highly supportive.

"This is important to me, Anand," she said, "it gives me so much pleasure and I am using my time in a way I enjoy. Surely you can't begrudge me that?"

"Who is begrudging you anything? There is no need for this... playing with metal and baubles at the expense of your family... neglecting us."

"The kids are not protesting. They like it."

"Well, I am. I don't like all this."

"Anand, I am not neglecting anyone. The kids are grown-up and you are an adult. All of you can take care of yourselves. I have spent my life attending to the needs of everyone else. I need this time for myself. I am going to nurture myself."

She was surprised at the firmness in her voice.

He shook his head in disbelief. "Of all things... jewellery design? What does a woman like you, who loves books and music, and hardly wears any jewellery, want to do with designing jewellery?"

"A love for beauty and design and aesthetics can be translated into anything. I was always drawn to jewellery design."

"Humpf. You'll let the house go to seed if you carry on like this."

"You are working from home, Anand. You can help."

"I don't have the time."

"I'll do the best I can then, Anand. The rest will figure itself out."

"What's the use of all this? Who will buy your jewellery? What makes you think it will sell?"

Reena shrugged her shoulders. "We shall see."

• 4 •

A Tenacious Hold

Anand walked into the dining room, his eyes searching for the newspapers and the coffee. He inhaled deeply. "Ah, coffee, thanks, Reena," he said.

"Welcome," she murmured from the kitchen, not looking up, busy packing the office lunch for Amit and Vandana. Amit was dressed and Vandana was snoozing but she would soon be out of bed.

Reena had prepared *poha* for their breakfast.

Anand sat at the dining table and his face disappeared behind the newspaper.

Reena's mobile rang. She turned off the gas and ran to pick it up from the table. It was her mother, Sushama.

"Hello, Mom," said Reena, breathing hard.

Reena's servant, Murali, was on leave and his absence was eating into her time and patience. As she spoke, she wiped the sweat off her brow. The kitchen was a hot place.

"*Haan*, Reena, how are you?"

"Busy, Mom, you know, early morning rush... and Murali being on leave..."

"Housewives have to be busy like this... I understand."

There was no point telling her mother that Ms Reena Rajan was now a jewellery designer who sold under her own brand, 'Wired and Stoned'. Her mother supported her in her work but insisted that her first duty was as a housewife.

Reena bit her tongue. *I must not react sharply. I must understand my mother.*

"So, can I call you later?" Reena asked, running her hand through her hair. *God, my hair is sticky with sweat.*

Sushama's tone turned conspiratorial. "Where is Anand?"

"He's around. Having his coffee."

"Okay, okay, how nice, must be busy, say hello from me. Hope you made his coffee for him? How long is he here this time?" Though Anand worked from his home office, he travelled all over India for his business.

Sushama always assumed that Anand was busy. Men were supposed to be, even when they put their feet up and smoked in front of the TV.

"Yes, Mother, he is not busy, I will tell him... I did make it. Don't know, I think he leaves on Tuesday. Call you later..."

Sushama's tone softened to a whisper. "Listen, I have taken an appointment with Mr Gupta the astrologer, for Thursday. Good to know Anand is leaving on Tuesday. Don't have to say anything to him about this."

"Mother..."

"Keep yourself free on Thursday. Get your horoscope out. Bye."

Reena put the mobile on the table and murmured on the way to the kitchen, "Mom says Hi to you, Anand."

"Hi back to her. Hope she is well?" Anand looked up from behind the paper.

"Yes..." said Reena, picking up his coffee mug.

Amit and Vandana rushed out from their rooms.

"Hi Dad, when did you arrive?" Vandana put her arms around him and hugged him.

Amit smiled. "Hi, Dad," he said quietly.

"Hey kiddos, I arrived last night, good to see both of you. Ready for office?"

"Breakfast first... what is there, Mom? Hey, Mom, watch it..." Vandana steadied Reena's hand. Reena had almost dropped the bowl of fruit she was carrying.

"These days without Murali, very trying, huh, Mom? Let me help..." Amit entered the kitchen to bring the dishes out.

Reena nodded, she could not tell them she was thinking of how to get out of meeting the astrologer on Thursday.

But her mother could be quite tenacious.

• 5 •

Discordant Notes

Reena had to, on Sushama's insistence, accompany her to the astrologer. He lived in a three room flat on the third floor of a building in Paharganj. They climbed steep steps to huff and puff into a place with nondescript furniture, most probably bought from some cheap Punchkuin Road shop. This cluttered the small room, leaving hardly any space to manouvre.

The servant informed them that the astrologer, Mr Gupta, was in the drawing room.

"May we come in?" Reena had ventured, standing outside the drawing room door, feeling quite like a schoolgirl wanting audience with the principal.

"Please come in," he said, and as they walked in, his voice boomed a good afternoon. His English was impeccable.

He was sitting cross-legged on his sofa. He asked, "*Kya lengii aap*?" He was polite as well. They agreed to lemonade.

Sushama handed Reena's astrological chart over to him.

The eyes were clear and piercing despite the folds of skin around them. "What do you want to know?" he asked, looking at it.

Sushama said, "I am concerned. There are too many ego clashes between Reena and her husband, and I fear the worst." Her voice faltered over the word. "Divorce?"

Reena was unconcerned. If her mother chose to believe the nonsense of an astrologer over a reality that existed, well, she was welcome. Her mother refused to understand her, and had dragged her to this place. As if his predictions could solve matters.

Mr Gupta began to speak. Reena watched her mother leaning forward, straining to hear every word.

"*Beti*," he said to her, "make notes. Come back to me after some months and let me know if what I have said is true."

Reena pulled out a small notebook from her handbag, opened it and started writing on the page. She felt once again in school, a little girl taking orders, doing what was required of her, erasing herself.

"*Beti*," he said again, "relationships survive and prosper only if you want them to. You have to want them to work."

What the hell was he talking about? She worked hard enough at everything. Trapped in a situation she wanted none of, she looked up angrily. "Mother, I have a meeting to attend."

Mr Gupta said, "*Beti*, you have come here with a purpose in mind. You will be glad to know that despite the discord, your marriage will survive."

Sushama heaved a sigh of relief. "She has too much pride," she said.

Mr Gupta looked at Reena. "Each individual is different. And changes. Your husband and you have changed in the course of the years. Don't be impatient."

"That is what I keep telling her," said Sushama.

"Oh, Mother!" Reena stamped her foot.

The old man spoke, "This is my second marriage. I have differences with my wife, but I consciously choose not to fight. Why do we fight? Our egos clash. And love, which creates compassion and understanding, is not there anymore to tell our egos to go take a walk."

Reena looked at the door. "I have to go," she said.

"Shanti, beti, shanti," he said.

As Reena hurried out of the room, she heard him tell Sushama, "Don't worry, better sense will prevail."

Outside, Reena stopped so that her mother could catch up with her. There was no point in rushing anywhere.

"No divorce, Reena, he said! That's all I wanted to hear."

"Now fate can take its course?" asked Reena, irritated.

Sushama gave her a watery smile. Her headstrong daughter did not realize the importance of marriage.

• 6 •

Forging an Identity

That Reena was trying to forge an identity of her own after so many years spent as a housewife, was something that stuck in Anand's gullet.

"There is no need for all this. Anyone would think you had time hanging on your hands. There are enough things for you to attend to, after all, you keep complaining of how tired you are..."

Reena wanted to throw a fit. Why did she have to *explain* to Anand? Did he ever have to explain to her his need to work or to relax with the newspaper or go out with friends? Why did he now begrudge her this desire to express herself?

She took a deep breath, and said, "Anand, I get tired because of the humdrum of all the things to do. I need some creative excitement, a challenge. All of you are busy with things you want to do. Look at the way you talk about a new project. There is so much fervour in your voice. I have never asked you why you need a new project to sink your teeth into every time, never said that I need you around me..."

"I pay the bills through this work. I can't take it easy at home."

Reena ignored the barb. Both of them knew that she never 'took it easy' at home, there were thousands of things to attend to, mundane everyday things that had to be done. It was an age-old argument that had no solution.

So often she had said, "Housewives need to be paid. Then their work will carry worth in tangible terms." But she did not want to get into that rigmarole. It tired her, when all she wanted to do was focus her energies on her next design.

"So, if the work goes well, I will also be paying bills... and we can both *take it easy* at home." She could not help being bitchy, finally.

"I am scared for you, for this is not a regular 9 to 5 job. It is a business that requires you to travel into the recesses of Delhi's manufacturing and industrial areas, seedy *mohallas* and narrow alleyways..."

"I have to do that to find my craftsmen and source my products. Okay, I will be careful, carry my mobile; let the family know where I am. I understand your concern."

I understand, she thought to herself, *and am trying hard to make you understand as well.*

II

II

◆ 7 ◆

The Big Jump

Even in the most educated and well-meaning of homes, a woman requires a fiery and independent spirit to battle traditional approaches and ideas. And if a woman is young and vulnerable, she often suffers the out-dated demands of not only the men, but also from the torch-bearers of tradition, the older Indian women.

Reena's thoughts strayed to Sanjay Singh and his wife. Sanjay Singh, the jewellery seller at Paharganj, was the young man who had introduced her to the tricks of the trade when she entered into the business of jewellery design two years ago. Neeru, his young wife, had welcomed Reena and Anjali, the beautician, into their home on the first day of their meeting.

Some days after they met, Reena had heard that Neeru was expecting. Sanjay was beside himself with joy. He had brought a box of *motichoor laddoos* for Reena and her family.

~

Three months into her pregnancy, Neeru had jumped off the terrace of her home, the narrow two-storey building in Paharganj.

It was rumoured that Sanjay's mother had forced Neeru to get an ultrasound at some shady clinic, where they had been informed that Sanjay and Neeru's first-born would be a girl. Sanjay's mother had been taking good care of Neeru till this time, telling her that she looked forward to a grandson. After the visit to the clinic, she had begun heckling Neeru to abort the child.

In those few days that her mother-in-law was with her, Neeru, simple and innocent, began to believe that she was responsible for a great calamity that would befall the family if she gave birth to a girl-child. She had climbed to the terrace at dead of night and jumped.

Sanjay had gone to Lucknow, to repay a loan he had taken from a friend at the start of his business. Meanwhile, not wanting to leave Neeru alone, he had especially called his mother from the village to take care of her daughter-in-law.

He had come home to find his wife was dead.

His mother had cursed Neeru, told Sanjay it was good he was rid of her, a woman who would bear only girls. She wanted him to marry again, but Sanjay, crazed by what had happened, fought with his mother and sent her back to the village. He withdrew into himself and threw himself into his work. He sold off his house in Paharganj and moved into a friend's small one-room flat.

"What will I do with a home now?" he had asked Reena when she had rushed there on hearing the news.

Reena had been filled with anguish and a sense of helplessness. It was not just another tale one read in the paper. This had happened to someone she had seen and talked with, a sweet girl who had smiled shyly at her and told her she was expecting a child and how happy she was, the joy visible in her shining eyes. And now she was dead, a death caused by no fault of her own.

They called it suicide. Neeru's mother-in-law even said that Neeru had been crazy in the head; that was why she had jumped. No one said the truth, that Indian society did not place any value on the girl-child. Sons were nurtured and loved, and daughters were suffered, or at best tolerated.

Reena, crying over the death of Neeru, had said to Anand, "Men do as they wish, and women do what men wish."

Anand had quietly said, an arm around her shoulder, "You are being unfair, Reena. It was her mother-in-law who instigated her."

Sanjay's mother had gone back to the village in Punjab to live with her elder son. She had been unable to convince her younger son to marry again.

~

The doorbell rang and Reena opened the door.

"*Namaste*, Madamji, please give me the car keys," said Sanjay Singh. He was now Reena's manager and driver; in many ways, her right-hand man.

"Good morning, you are really early today, Sanjay?" asked Reena. Even the newspaper had not arrived, he was that early.

"Yes, Madam, Amit *bhaiya* had asked me to come early and clean the car from inside today."

"Oh, okay. Just a moment," said Reena, and stepped inside. She walked the hallway to her bedroom on the left, hands in her dressing-gown pocket, to fetch the car keys.

Another day had begun. Life went on, despite births and deaths, she thought wryly as she handed Sanjay the keys and gave him a small smile.

He did not smile back. He had lost the ability to smile the day when he learnt his wife had plunged to her death and he was not there to save her. He left, and Reena entered the kitchen to make a cup of tea.

She removed from the cupboard a big, orange cup with the design of a galloping black horse. She called it her Black Beauty cup, and she took it out on special days, when she needed extra comfort.

No sugar? The thought crossed her mind. Then she stirred half-a-teaspoon into the cup. The morning needed some relief, some dose of sweetness.

• 8 •

Tea, Termites and Fish

Reena found a certain pleasure in making an early morning tea for herself, boiling the water and dipping a Tajmahal tea bag in her special orange cup, straining the milk and dropping in a half-opened clove of green cardamom for its special flavor.

She pushed her long black hair back as she looked out of the 6th floor window, tea cup in hand. The breeze on her neck was cool and delicious. She could see children running for the school bus, couples out for a morning walk. Labourers were hard at work on beautifying the boundary wall of the society that housed the apartment buildings.

The apartments, called 'Seaside View Apartments', are in the heart of Delhi. Delhi is in the heart of India, with no sea in sight for hundreds of miles around. But the man who had first envisaged these apartments was from Mumbai, a sea port. He had wanted to build in Mumbai but had been unable to do so for some unexplained reason.

He bought land in Delhi, built the apartments here, but gave them the name he had envisaged for them right from the time he had dreamt of building them. It's like you want a daughter and decide to name her Roshni. But you have a son. What do you do then with the dream name? You name him Roshni. And leave it to the world to figure out why.

Watching the workers, she grimaced. She had fought with the society's secretary a few days ago. She had complained about how the termites were infesting one of her bathrooms, and he said that she would have to attend to the matter herself since the society had no funds. She had argued that they pay a hefty amount for maintenance, but her words fell on deaf ears.

And now he was busy getting the boundary wall 'decorated' with barbed wire and glass shards for protection. He'd had the trees that grew near the wall cut down to create more parking space for more cars.

This was where the funds went, and no one had the time to protest.

Neither did she have the time; she did not want to spend her hours embroiled in the apartments' society politics.

But she had given him a piece of her mind. "We will soon have a building that is beautiful outside, but ready to fall, eaten up by termites from the inside."

To which he had said, "Reena *jiiii*," his voice dripping with extra politeness, "we have asked structural engineers to look into the matter and they will send us a report. We will do then what needs to be done. You know all this needs a lot of funds. Members have to be ready to pay."

She looked down at the teacup. The cardamom floated in the last sip of tea. She placed the cup on the table and walked to the front door. She would fetch the paper and read it for a while before she made Anand's coffee.

He had returned once again from a business trip last night and gone straight to bed, mumbling something about having had enough of travelling for a while.

She unlatched the front door. The newspaper, as usual, was lying on the front door step.

Next to it, winking at her in the sun, lay a big *Hilsa* fish.

♦ 9 ♦

A Good Beginning

What the f...!

"*Arre, kaun hai*? Who's there?" Reena called out to no one in particular.

A boy dressed in shorts and a half-sleeved shirt peeped around the wall that led to the landing. "*Memsahib*, you ordered the fish, *na*?"

"No, I did not." Reena glared at him. "Come here," she said. "Pick the damned thing up."

"But, *Memsahib*, Flat No. 69, this one, *na*?"

"*Na, nahin, nyet*, not," she said, pointing her finger to the neighbour's flat on the left. So it was ordered by the couple who had moved in next door into the Topsy-Turvy Flat. Reena and family called it the Topsy-Turvy Flat because of the number 69, and because no one stayed there peacefully for very long.

"*Memsahib*, sorry!" He ran over and picked up the fish.

Reena watched him drop it at the front door of Flat No. 69.

"Ring the bell," she said, "and let them know."

He rang the bell, then stood there and waited. She watched him, and waited.

The door opened and a young man in pajamas and spectacles stood inside. Reena could figure out that

♦ 48 ♦

though handsome, his face was already fleshy and in just a few years would become a round blob.

"Ah," he said, looking at the fish, "ah, *Ilish!*" He called out to someone inside, "Pro... teeksha... O, Proteeksha..." The way he said the name, it sounded like Proteeksha. He was pronouncing it the Bengali way, she realized, turning the *a* into an *o*.

There was no response to his call. He shrugged.

"*Sahib*, you ordered this..." The young boy picked up the fish and held it out. Its metallic silver scales shone in the early morning light like a knight's armour.

"Yes." He gingerly took the fish into his two hands like a prized possession. "Yes, I did."

The boy grinned, gave a quick *salaam*, and ran off.

~

So, now we have a Bengali neighbour, thought Reena. She hated to cook fish, but liked to eat it occasionally in restaurants and at the homes of friends. Anand had settled for lamb and chicken dishes at home once he realized that Reena did not like cooking fish.

Reena watched her part-time maid, Parvati, walking up the hallway towards her flat. Parvati came in everyday for a couple of hours to help Reena cope with the household chores. Murali had returned to the village to look after his ailing father. His father had died of kidney failure, and now his mother was ill. There was no hope for Murali's return. However, Reena had been unable to find a full-time servant to take his place.

Reena pounced on Parvati. "First, clean the doorstep."

The Bengali neighbour looked up from the fish in his hands. "Hello, just a moment," he said.

Now she had to wait again. Reena tapped an impatient foot. As she waited, Parvati flicked the mop across the doorstep and around the newspaper, and disappeared inside. Reena frowned. She would make Parvati pour some disinfectant over the spot and clean it again, later. She missed Murali, who had been a good servant. She never had to tell him how she liked things done.

The neighbour returned soon enough, without the fish. His hands were wet, and he shook them in the air, then wiped them on the sides of his *kurta*.

"Hello," he said, "I am Anirban, Anirban Dasgupto. Sorry, my wife is not well, she is still sleeping."

Oh, so it *was* a couple. "Hello," said Reena, "I am Reena Rajan."

He looked at the nameplate beside the front door. It read *Vardharajan*.

She could see the question mark forming in his head.

"Rajan is your husband?"

"No, he is Anand."

"Then..."

"Well, the full name is Vardharajan, but we use the short form, bit much to write. But we don't want to lose the long name either. So we use it in places like the front door."

"Oh, I see. Your husband is Anand Vardharajan, but calls himself Anand Rajan. And you are Mrs Anand, but call yourself Mrs Rajan," he said, blinking his eyes behind his spectacles.

"Yes, you got it," said Reena, not wanting to argue with his convoluted logic. She picked up the paper, wanting to read the day's news. The maid was inside, cleaning the drawing room. Reena had to go in to keep an eagle eye on her, making sure she did the corners. And she had to make Anand's coffee.

And here this man was discussing names and surnames with her, wasting her precious Spring morning.

"Please excuse me, Mr Dasgupta," she said.

"It is not Dasgupta," he said.

"Huh?" said Reena.

"Mrs Rajan, it is Dasgupto," he said. "Das... gupto."

"Yes," she looked pointedly at the newly placed brass nameplate outside Flat No. 69, which read A. Dasgupta, engraved in black calligraphy. "Dasgupta, so you told me."

"No, Mrs... er... Rajan, what I am telling you is 'Dasgupto', with an 'o'."

"But... on your name plate... it's an 'a'."

"Yes, Ma'am, we write Dasgupta and pronounce it Dasgupto."

"Oh, like in *rosogulla*. I mean... *gullo*."

"*Hain,* yes, you like the sweet?"

"My husband does, he stayed in Kolkata as a student. I am more of a *gulabjamun* person."

"You are more North Indian, right?"

"No, no, nothing like that..." Reena protested, wondering how she was caught up in all this, struggling like a fish caught in a net.

She looked down and saw her slippers. They had thin straps of silver, with scales painted on them. She had never looked at them this closely before. "Er... excuse me," she said, "I have to go."

"Of course. I will ask my wife, Proteeksha, to meet you sometime."

Reena nodded.

Anirban said, a big smile lighting up his face, "How lucky that a fish, that also *Ilish maach*, has introduced us to each other. It is a good beginning."

The fish scales on her slippers winked at her in the morning rays of the sun.

The Scales

Reena looked hard at the scales again. Well, she need not have weighed herself. She knew for each of the three months of Winter, she had put on three kilos of weight, so now the scales tipped horribly to add nine kilos more to her previous reading of three months ago.

She did not weigh herself everyday nor did she weigh herself once a month or anything like that. Her weighing in was seasonal, she thought wryly, or impulsive, maybe.

It could also be due to the impending danger of having to reveal.

Spring was here, Summer was coming, and in the sweltering heat you did nothing but reveal, reveal, reveal. That was the only way to beat the heat, to expose skin to air, or wear the thinnest and finest of *saris* and *salwars* to let the air enter your body through the fine weave. Even if it was hot air, it was air.

At the moment, the air refused to enter her lungs. She could not take in the reading on the scales. That was because her stomach was in the way, blocking the numbers.

She stood on the scales, then took the mobile from her pocket and messaged Vandana who was in the next room, to come read the scales for her. Thank god it was a Saturday and Vandana was at home.

Vandy came into the room, chomping a kebab. "These are good, Ma, want a bite?"

Reena did. No, she didn't. Why did life have to rub salt in the wound? Or sprinkle salt on the burn?

"Vandy, just put the kebab down and read my weight for me, I can't see the scales."

Vandana pushed the last morsel into her mouth and wiped her hands on a towel lying on the bed. Reena grimaced but decided not to admonish her daughter for using such a large towel just for wiping her hands.

Vandy waltzed over to Reena and peered. "Well, Mom, it's just a wonderful 81 kg."

Eighty plus one, Eighty-one, 81. That was hardly a wonderful number, read it or say it any which way. She had been 72 kg before Winter and adipose began to settle in. Covered with sweaters and shawls, the weight had been well hidden.

Reena was ready to cry. "Look again, poochikins," she said, "maybe it's less?"

"Mother... what is a kilo less or more, consider the larger picture, *na*?"

"Please co-operate, Vandy, see if the zero is positioned okay? It may be skewed to read more?" Reena stepped off the scale.

"It's fine, Mom," Vandana said. "Read the writing on the wall, you just need to get those inches off. Okay, me going for some more kebab. Should I get you an apple?"

Reena knew her daughter was being helpful, but it was a bit mean not to offer her a kebab. She looked mournfully at her stomach and saw the rolls. Ugh, she thought, now back to apples and oranges and goodbye to kebabs and *tandoori rotis*.

She would have to take matters in hand. She would give up oil, meat and sugar. She would begin with sugar. From tomorrow, she would take no sugar in her tea.

No sweets at all, especially no *gujiya* for *Holi*, even if *Holi* was the day after tomorrow... and even though she had an absolute weakness for the sweet filled with *khoya*, cardamoms, almonds, dried coconut, and even though it was so deliciously crunchy.

What was *Holi* without *gujiya*, but she would have to give it a miss.

She contemplated shifting the date of the beginning of her sacrifice. Perhaps she could do all this after *Holi*? What were two more days?

She steeled herself. This would be a true test, and she would begin from tomorrow. She thought of how she hardly had any sugar in any case, now she would be really giving it up. Morning tea without sugar would be crazy, but she would go through with it.

She had done it before, hadn't she? She had lost weight and brought it down to the 72 kg after spending a week at a yoga centre.

When her young yoga teacher had called in for a review, she had answered happily, "You will be glad to know that I have been maintaining my weight."

His voice had been cutting, sharp, unyielding. "Madam, you are supposed to *lose* more weight, not *maintain* it."

She had realized the truth of his statement. Yet sweet things like *gujiya* had called, and she could not bring herself to give tea up forever. So she had gone from 'maintaining' her weight to the stage of her clothes 'straining' against her weight.

"I shall give up sugar and sweets from tomorrow," she vowed. "I shall overcome, I shall say 'yes' to 'no'. No, thank you, I don't drink tea; No thank you, I don't eat *gujiya*; No, thank you, I don't eat mangoes..."

◆ II ◆

Scheming Gods

The gods were scheming against her.

It was really strange. When she was making her morning tea and Anand's coffee, she found a single *motichoor kesar laddoo*, lying on the shelf, dripping its sweetness into a polythene bag.

Who could have got a single *laddoo* into the home? She thought Amit may have had some *puja* at office and brought it from there. He must have forgotten to mention it.

Reena was not so fond of *laddoos*. But she was hungry in the morning and had not had any breakfast. The sight of the *laddoo* filled her with sudden want.

She did not think twice and just reached for it. She popped it into her mouth and as its delectable sweetness filled her mouth, she sighed, and was in heaven.

She could wash this sweetness down with some milk. That's how people used to breakfast in certain Haryana villages, she had heard. She had heard that people ate *laddoos* mixed with yoghurt as well. Oh, the sweetness of it all. It was like pancakes with milk.

Now if anyone went, "Omigod, how can anyone eat a *laddoo* and *like that*, for breakfast...!" she would definitely shut them up. They made fun of this just because it was a village thing, she thought. Now if someone had said that in Boston people did something like this, it would become the fashion in New Delhi, she just knew it.

She had cheated first thing in the morning, but then the fates were to blame. Never before had she found something like this in the kitchen, a single piece, asking her to break her vow.

And strangely enough, for breakfast she had wanted to have bagels with jam. She had not had jam for a long time. So, a *laddoo* on her plate instead.

Well, maybe the gods were not scheming against her. Maybe they were just listening to her in their own odd way. For, they had given her jam too, some time earlier.

~

One afternoon, she had received a surprise call from Amit. She had been standing in front of her wardrobe mirror, checking to see whether her new *kameez* made her appear slimmer. She reached into her *salwar* pocket for the mobile when it rang, and sat on the bed.

Amit usually did not call from office. Perhaps he was calling regarding the new lock they wanted installed. Both Amit and Vandana had lost their house keys one after the other, so Anand had asked Amit to arrange for a new lock for the front door.

His voice came onto the line. It was not his normal voice. It was accented. He seemed to be trying a sophisticated American drawl, if such a thing was possible.

Reena's brow puckered. *Now what?* she thought.

"Jams," he said.

"Jams?" Reena asked, perplexed. "What kind of jams?" Her mind raced, but his voice was relaxed, so she knew it was not a traffic jam.

In any case, he would not call her regarding a traffic jam in the middle of the afternoon. He was not expected home at this time.

She remembered that he had said that his boss had gone to Milan and Dubai, so he was doing a couple of site visits. He had also dressed rather casually, not his usual plain office shirts and formal pants. It was obvious that he was having an office lunch in Khan or HKV or Saket, someplace where jams were also part of the deal.

No one in Reena's family relished jam, only she did. She loved marmalade most of all. But her son calling her in the afternoon from work and asking her about jams? That was a bit much.

"Er... jams?" she asked again.

"Mom... should I get you some jams... you like jams... marmalade?" His voice kind of drifted off into uncertainty.

"Yes, marmalade, of course, and strawberry, cranberry, blueberry, whatever... and while you are about it, don't forget the lock as well." Reena knew how to make the most of an unprecedented opportunity. It was not everyday her son called up and asked her if he should buy her not jam, but a variety of jams!

"These are special. One has cinnamon and rum, another has figs..."

Oh joy, sighed Reena. *Why make my mouth water so.*

"Amit, thanks, sounds too good," she said.

"Yes, Mom, I thought as much. I'll get the lock as well," he drawled.

How compliant and willing.

She placed the mobile on the side table. Then she burst out laughing. He must be hitting on someone behind a shop counter, someone selling jams. And she could be of foreign origin or someone he needed to impress a lot, accent and all.

The games one played to court! And then when the mask slipped, oh, such heartache. But all was fair in love and war. And he was young, handsome and not committed.

She would quiz him and tease him a bit on his return home. Meanwhile, she looked forward to many days of sweet breakfasts.

The gods were really indulging her sweet tooth. Why else this sudden gift of jams? They must know that a couple of toasts with jam for breakfast could not wreak much havoc.

Reena stood in front of the wardrobe mirror once again. She sucked in her stomach. She looked so much slimmer in the new *kameez*.

III

The Coming of Harinmoy Banerjee

Harinmoy Banerjee came into Reena's life just by chance. He rang her doorbell instead of the neighbours'.

"Oh, no, now what?" said Reena and stood up from the sofa to attend it. She was quite sick of attending doorbells and hoped to employ a full-time servant soon to attend to them.

"Madam Prerna, is it not, dear?"

Dear? She must have heard wrong. She shook her head to clear it, and of course, to also say No.

"You are...?" asked the stranger at the door.

She did not give her name. She did not trust her name with anyone who rang her doorbell just like that.

"Aap kaun?" she asked, not being very polite because he looked gross. Heavy-faced and dark-skinned, he stood there chewing *supari*, his cheeks full and lips wet. He wore a white hat with a black bandana tied around it and had a black moustache that lay untrimmed across his upper lip.

"My card, Madam..." His fat fingers held a visiting card that he shoved under her nose. 'Harinmoy Banerjee, investigator, detective, SS.'

"The SS is for Super Sleuth, everyone asks me, you see," he said, his grimy finger between shirt collar and neck, then the same finger straightening his shirt across his midriff.

Reena looked at him. He looked peculiar, white hat, black goggles, orange scarf and yellow shirt with white pants. The pointed white shoes were the best.

He asked, leaning forward a bit, "Madam, you are not Madam Prerna?"

"No Prerna here." Reena handed back his card.

"No, keep the card, you may need it, is it not, dear?"

She wanted to fling the card to the ground, but stopped. Why the hell did he think she might need his services? And what was with this *'dear'* thing?

"It is, I think, her name is Prateeksha..." he said now, biting his lower lip, the *supari* thickening his voice.

"She lives next door," said Reena, suddenly curious as to why Prateeksha needed the services of such a man.

"Then, sorry Madam, I have pressed the wrong button," he said, straightening up.

You sure have, thought Reena, *not one... but several.*

She was not in the best of moods. The clothes had not returned from the dry-cleaners despite repeated phone calls to the shop, and she needed to wear her green and gold Maheshwari sari the next day. Her leg was giving her trouble again after a brief respite of a couple of months, and there was no one to massage it for her.

Reena looked him up and down. Yuck, you never knew what some people liked or associated with.

She wouldn't be seen dead dealing with someone like him. Prateeksha was welcome to him.

She began to shut the door when he said, "Madam, may I have some water?"

Now water cannot be refused by anyone to anyone, even if you are nursing a sore head and a sorer leg. This is just not done in India.

"Fine," she said, and turned to fetch him some water.

When she returned with it, he had stepped inside. She was taken aback and chided herself. Why had she not shut the door on him before entering the kitchen?

How often had Anand warned her about people like this, telling her to be careful about shutting the front door.

She was glad Anand was home, though he was fast asleep in the bedroom.

"Oh," she said, "here is the water."

He sipped it slowly. "Thank you, Madam," he said. "This is a nice flat. Are all flats like this?"

"Yes," she said, and wanted to say, *now vamoose.*

"Who is it, Reena?" Anand was in the hallway, his hair ruffled and his eyes still swollen with sleep.

"Some guy looking for Prateeksha... Dasgupta's wife in Flat 69, do you know her?"

Anand said, "Yes, our neighbour, pretty young thing."

Reena's face flushed. She had not met Prateeksha as yet, though she had met her husband. So she was a PYT, was she? Anand did not have to be so frank in front of this strange man.

Harinmoy removed his goggles and stared into her flushed face. Reena did not like that at all.

He then looked at Anand and extended his card. "Myself, Harinmoy Banerjee, Sir. Hot day, is it not, dear?"

Anand said, "Let me show you Prateeksha's house..." and led him out, shutting the front door firmly behind them.

• 13 •

Butterfly, Dog, SS

Reena returned from the local market and stood waiting near the lift, two huge bags filled with provisions on either side of her. *Whatever else one does, food always comes first,* she thought. She wiped the sweat from her brow with her small, embroidered handkerchief. This was her latest 'thing'.

She had been a tissue user for a long time, but now she was following her latest craze, the desire to use pretty handkerchiefs. *One has small indulgences, such as tea and hankies, and these have to be a part of life, otherwise...* She looked ruefully at the two bags, heavy and bulging with her purchases.

The lift was taking its sweet time coming. Someone came up to her and said, "Hell-llo, Madam."

She looked at the man standing to her side. "Hello, Mr Banerjee," she said.

"Why the formality with me, Madam? I'm just Harinmoy to you. These are your packets?"

"Yes, my bags," she said.

She was tired and her feet ached. Shopping in the sun was not a joke.

"You do whole month shopping today?" he smiled. His teeth were orange against his dark lips. She was sure he had a *supari* tucked in somewhere, which he would chew upon as soon as he stopped talking.

She wanted to tell him that a full house meant provisions that finished fast and had to be replenished with alarming alacrity.

"You live alone, I suppose," she said instead, wondering why she was talking with this fellow.

"Yes, Madam, I see you are SS yourself."

"You mean Super Sleuth like you?" She smiled at the idea.

"Ah, smiling, Madam, but it is serious, is it not, dear?"

Reena stopped smiling. *Oh god*, she thought, *this* dear *business, where the hell has he picked that up?*

"I am alone, Madam, that is why I can flit like a butterfly from job to job. My cases are all over India, you see. And may soon happen outside India too."

She imagined butterfly wings on this short, plump man in yellow shirt, bright blue pants and white patent leather shoes. Well, he was colourful, but she wasn't that sure of his wing-flapping abilities.

The lift arrived, with its customary 'ping'. Reena bent to pick up her bags.

Harinmoy said, "I am strong, Madam, please, let me..." and picked the bags up from their handles. She did not protest.

When they arrived on the 6th floor, he heaved the bags to her front door. She turned the key to the door and he brought the bags inside.

"Thank you," she said, "that is very kind of you..."

"No problem, Madam, Prateeksha's friend... also my friend."

"I am more her neighbour," she said, for she could hardly consider herself to be Prateeksha's friend.

She did not want to be rude. After all, he had helped her with the bags.

"Would you like some tea?" she asked.

"Yes, Madam," he said, and sat down on the sofa.

She had no choice now. Not wishing to enter her bedroom while this man sat on the drawing room sofa, she splashed some water on her face from the kitchen sink, dabbed her handkerchief over her face and put it on the counter. Then she filled the saucepan with water and placed it on the stove.

~

He took the first sip of the tea she made and said, "Aah! Madam, this tea is wonderful. Just like in my home town. No one makes it like this here, but you have done it, is it not, dear?"

Sitting opposite, Reena sipped her tea and smiled. Perhaps she had been quick to judge him.

"What is it with Prateeksha?" she asked. "Why are you working for her?"

Harinmoy took another sip of his tea and said, "Madam, it is all very fishy. Sad but true, food can make or break a house."

Reena sipped and waited.

Harinmoy took out a big red handkerchief, wiped his face, and returned it to his pant pocket.

"Madam, her husband, Mr Dasgupta, is lost. MIA. But I am on his tail." From his pant pocket, a bit of his handkerchief hung out like the tongue of a panting dog. "Yes, for her sake, I am sniffing him out."

"Oh, you mean he is not at home? But... I saw him..." said Reena.

"That must have been some time ago?"

"Er... actually... yes..."

"Now he is missing. And Madam Prateeksha is crying many tears. And she has employed me to get him back."

"Oh!" Reena had missed out on all this. Though, now that she thought about it, after the Fish on Doorstep incident, she had not seen any more of Anirban.

She made a face. "So he has run away? Usually, the women run away... they are often ill-treated..."

"Nowadays, men also run away... unhappiness has no gender, Madam."

"But why would he be unhappy in his own home? Newly married, at that?" Reena could not understand all this. The beginning of married life was all romance, differences cropped up later on.

"Sometimes a childhood love holds more value than the present one."

"Meaning? You mean to say that he loved someone else, but listened to his parents and had an arranged marriage?" She sighed. Men were all the same. They love someone, and marry someone else. "And now he has gone back to his childhood love?"

"You are right, dear!"

"Well, Prateeksha should be smarter, she should say good riddance."

"She loves him."

"But he loves another, in his village?"

"Yes."

"Who is she, do you know?" Reena had forgotten how hot it was, how tired she was.

"Not SHE, Madam, IT!"

"It? A eunuch? Unbelievable."

Harinmoy Banerjee's eyes glinted. "No, no, Madam, nothing is unbelievable. But... you are jumping to conclusions. Don't be so fast."

"What's IT, then?" Reena leaned forward.

"It is fish, Madam, simply fish."

"IT is fish? He has left his wife for *fish*?"

"Childhood love, Madam. His *Ilish maach*. He hungers for it."

"But... but... he has it here. I saw it here... the fish. He took it in."

"Prateeksha will have none of it. She told me he fought with her over the cooking of fish and the eating of fish. Then he left without a word and has not returned. Now, I have to find him."

"Oh, okay," said Reena, smoothing her hair.

"Okay, Madam, I will come again sometime for your excellent tea, thank you. I will tell you of my progress. Maybe you can give me some idea too, since you are SS also."

• 14 •

The Green Monster

Dariba Kalan is the jewellery making and shopping centre of Old Delhi. Now jewellery shops abound in all the local markets, in the upmarket shopping centres and the mushrooming malls. But there is a certain charm to this place with its noise and crowd, the hustle and bustle in the narrow street.

Reena was here with a purpose.

She was looking for a particular shop which had a jeweller who could craft her designs the way she wanted. The jeweller she had been working with had left for his hometown, telling her he would probably not return, for his mother had taken sick. She had been thrown into a quandary, but Sanjay had come to her rescue, saying that he knew someone who did exquisite work, and if she was lucky, he would still be around in his shop in Dariba. Reena had quickly scribbled the address of the shop on a piece of paper, for Sanjay did not have the phone number of this shop.

So she was here now, fervently hoping she would meet the man as she stepped into the shop.

"I am at the shop in Dariba," Reena messaged Anand.

Her mobile phone pinged.

"Good," Anand had messaged back. "My meeting is cancelled, so I am relaxing at home."

"Fine, then please let Parvati in, she said she would come in late today," she texted back, and looked up from her mobile into the weathered face of an old man with a long grey beard.

"Yes, Madam?" he asked.

"I am looking for Mian Murtaza," she said.

"I am Murtaza."

"Oh, thank god!" Reena pushed an unruly strand of hair off the nape of her sweaty neck.

"*Paani*, Madam?"

"*Haan*, cold, please."

An earthen water pot stood in the corner. He dipped a long-handled brass ladle into the pot, poured water into a steel glass, and handed Reena the glass, stooping a little as he did so.

Reena gulped down the water and then sat on the leatherite seat opposite the glass-topped wooden counter that displayed some necklaces, rings and pendants. She placed her satchel next to her and fished inside it for the designs which she spread out onto the glass top.

He looked at the sketches and said, "You have some work for me?"

"Yes, Sanjay sent me to you."

He shook his head, a little sadly, "Ah, Sanjay."

He reached into his *kurta* pocket and took out his glasses and perched them on his nose. Reena looked at him and did the same, fishing her glasses out and placing them on her nose.

They smiled at each other.

He peered at the designs. Reena's heart lurched for a moment. Maybe he was too old, incapable even. She picked up one of the designs and handed it to him.

He gave it a glance and said, "Not a problem."

"May I see some of your work?" she asked.

"Of course," he said, "let me show you something like the work you want."

He returned with a small brooch. It was a beautiful bird, with a red and blue enamelled body, and wings of fine gold wire. Reena gasped when she saw it, but quickly straightened her face. He must not know her delight for he would up his charges.

"Quite good," she said. "But my design is contemporary, quite different, you can do it?"

"Yes, when do you want this one?" he said, pointing to the first design she had shown him.

They spent a long time discussing details of costing, materials, delivery schedules and the process of payment. It was four in the afternoon by the time Reena was done.

"I am leaving," she messaged Anand. "Will be there in an hour."

"Alright, I should be done by then," he messaged back.

"Oh, where are you?"

"Will tell you on your return. Travel safe."

~

Reena was exhausted but happy when she entered her home. "Anand..." she called out.

"Right here," he said, looking up from the paper he was reading, sitting on the sofa.

She fetched herself some cold water from the fridge. She sat on the sofa and kicked off her sandals. "What a relief! I found Mian Murtaza, now I only hope he delivers the goods in time."

"He is preparing a sample for you?"

"No, a piece each, of the 5 items."

Anand's eyebrows shot up. "You are taking a chance, aren't you?"

"Instinct. I don't doubt the quality of his work." She sipped the water and asked him, "So where were you? The meeting happened?"

"No, I was next door, at Prateeksha's."

The colour drained from Reenas face. "Prateeksha's? And what, may I ask, were you doing there?"

"Relax, Reena, I am not running away with her or something. She was having a problem with her laptop so she called this nice Uncle from next door to help her fix it."

"And did you fix it?"

"Yes, it was a major glitch."

"How long were you there?"

"Oh, just for a couple of hours. She gave me lemonade to drink while I worked at the problem."

"Lucky her that you are so technology-savvy and available," said Reena. She tried to remember whether she had taken her blood pressure medicine in the morning before leaving for Dariba.

"Her lemonade is nothing like yours."

"Well, that's some consolation," said Reena and stood up. Her legs ached. She told herself that she would not walk off in a huff, she would not get angry, there was no reason to, she was making a mountain out of a molehill...

She took small, measured steps toward the bedroom.

"So it was a good day on the whole?" asked Anand, following her in.

"I just met an old man, Anand, and I only hope he does the work well," she said. She turned to him, "Oh, my legs ache. Do you think you could massage them once I lie down?"

"Of course, darling," he said, grinning. "Anything else you want me to do? Something further up?"

"No, just a leg massage." She could not bring herself to smile at him, forgive him so soon.

Reena lay on the bed and closed her eyes. She thought she must make sure that Anand did not frequent the flat next door too often. As she drifted off to sleep, the touch of Anand's fingers soothing her feet, she dreamed of Prateeksha flying away with a flock of fish-shaped birds.

15

The Exercycle

Reena sat on the exercycle.

It had been standing around for some years, occupying a corner of the bedroom. Reena had not used it at all. She had bought it at a time when she was very enthused with the idea of building her leg muscles through cycling.

Now she had decided to use it. She had to do something about her weight and the usual type of disciplines employed for this, namely dieting and walking, had been unable to yield any eye-popping results.

Losing half a kilo was not the intention, she had to lose at least 10 kg to get back into shape.

No wonder Anand has begun to eye that silly girl next door, Reena thought. *She is slim, even if she is stupid. She has to be stupid if her husband manages to go off somewhere without her and does not leave any clue as to where he is.*

Reena cycled harder. "She is stupid, isn't she?" she said aloud.

"Who?" Anand lay on the bed, reading the newspaper. What he found in the newspaper that could occupy two hours of his time everyday was beyond Reena, but after so many years of marriage, she had given up trying to find out.

~

As long as Anand did not go next door again, she thought. And then bring the girl back with him also for lunch or dinner, with her saying, "Auntie, how I love your *aloo-paranthas.*"

Once, Prateeksha had said, "I wish *he* (her husband who had disappeared) would settle for vegetarian food." Then she had burst into tears.

Another time, she had said, "Uncle is so kind to bring me here." Anand had then patted her back comfortingly. Rather comfortably, Reena thought.

Reena had warned Anand about bringing her over but he kept saying, "Poor girl, poor girl, Reena you must understand what she is going through... put yourself in her place..."

She had almost said, "You are deserting me now, aren't you, me the fat sinking ship, so I am in her place really..." but restrained herself. This was not how independent and feisty women thought and felt. She would be proud and accepting of her body. Anand either loved her the way she was, or... well, the *or* was not worth thinking about.

~

"Who?" asked Anand again.

She slowed down her cycling, took a deep breath, and said, "I am talking about Prateeksha, who else? Stupid girl, letting her husband go..."

"She did not; Reena, have a heart. She is sobbing away because he has left her and gone. Who would leave such a lovely girl and go..."

"Yeah, who would?" Reena said bitterly and began cycling madly, her feet whirring, sweat forming on her upper lip.

She would show them all. She would get so slim and svelte that heads would turn when she passed; she still had it in her. *But it was an uphill climb...*

Anand said, "But he did leave, and that Harinmoy is being paid a packet to track him down. The man should not be hanging around here. He should be somewhere else, chasing him..."

"He is doing what he can, Anand, he knows his job."

"I am sure he does, hanging around the ladies all the time. And you really do encourage him a lot."

You never know, I might need him too, she thought to herself. "Anand, he is a hardworking, lonely man."

"And my heart weeps," Anand mocked, clutching his chest.

"He meets me because I make good tea, and because he thinks I am a potential SS."

"My god, you joining Hitler...??"

"No, Anand," Reena said slowly, "SS as in Super Sleuth."

"Ouch," said Anand, his eyebrows wriggling like black caterpillars.

"This is serious, why must you think of all this as a joke..."

"Oh, I see. If I did not know you so well, I would have thought there was a rip-roaring romance between you two. The way you go, 'Harin, have some tea... have some biscuits...'," he grinned.

Reena did not know whether to smile or sigh. She was too old for romance, now?

"I am just being hospitable," she said.

"It's okay, don't get defensive, I know you have better taste in men."

"And you? What about your taste?"

"Well, I have no taste for men," he teased.

"I know," she said, impatient. She took her feet off the pedals, which spun on their own for a while.

"So, then what? I love you, you know that."

She blushed and began to cycle madly again. "You do?"

"Yes, now get off that high horse and come into my arms," he said.

Reena said, "I have another ten minutes left..."

"That is the problem. You kill all the romance nowadays." Anand looked down at his newspaper again.

Reena jumped off the cycle. "I'll go make some tea," she said, smoothing her *salwar* along her legs. Her thighs were already feeling tighter.

Then pain shot up her left knee. "Ouch," she said, clutching at it, "there goes my knee..." Her face contorting with the pain, she held on to the wall for support, hobbling towards the bed. Anand clambered off the bed to help her, taking her arm so she could lean against him.

"Lie down, I'll bring you some tea," he said. "You had to come into my arms somehow. The gods sometimes do listen to me."

She looked at him, her eyes widening. He had changed. The earlier, less-liberated Anand would never have made tea.

16

Try Sharing the Bananas

The physiotherapist, Dr Brij Bhushan, was young, and he smiled. He came from Uttarakhand, the hills above Delhi. He lacked the Delhi suaveness, but his tone was earnest.

"How are you?" he asked Reena, taking the tea and biscuits she served him. Then he smiled again.

For the last week, Reena had visited the local physiotherapy centre for the IFT and Ultrasound treatment, but the pain persisted.

Now it shot up the inside of her left knee.

She grimaced. "I have called you. How do you think I'll be?"

"No problem," he smiled, "you will be okay."

"I can only hope." She joined her palms and fingers together in supplication to an unknown god.

"I'll start from tomorrow. You will recover." He placed the cup and saucer on the table. "Have you heard of Kamaal baba?"

"Baba who?"

"He is a fellow who used to have a show on TV and has quite a following."

"Why?"

"Well, people come to him for medicine for their ailments, and he gives them the medicine."

"Does his treatment work?"

"Don't know how or why it would, but going by the following he has, it seems people will swallow anything." He grinned.

"Like?" The pain shot higher up her leg and Reena gripped her left knee hard.

"Well, if someone like you complained of leg pain, and went up to him for a cure, he would ask, 'How many bananas have you eaten in the last week?'

"Suppose you answer that you have eaten one. He will ask then, 'Did you eat it alone or share it with someone?' Suppose you say, 'I ate it alone.' So he will nod his head and say, 'Buy a dozen bananas, eat two and give the rest to ten people. God's *kripa,* his benevolence, on you, will be restored. Follow this treatment for a month. Your pain will go.'

"You will nod and go away and do what he suggests. If your pain somehow goes away, you will sing his praises. If it does not, you will think you did not do something right. You *may* doubt him, but then, with so many believers..."

"We are cured if we eat and share bananas?" Reena hobbled to the kitchen with the teacup and saucer. They wobbled in her hands. If only bananas could help, she thought.

"He has many kinds of cures. His followers swear by him." Dr Bhushan stood up to leave, brushing crumbs from his shirt.

"I don't think I could listen to him without laughing." Reena smiled as she hobbled back into the living room.

"A lot of it is a mind thing. Should I put fenugreek seeds on your toes when I come tomorrow?" he asked her at the front door.

"A Kamaal baba remedy?"

"Oh no, something I read on the net. It may work."

"You just do the IFT, Ultrasound, and the exercises with me. If nothing works, then we will consider fenugreek seeds."

"Madam, even if you don't eat the bananas, stay smiling."

Reena smiled, held her stomach and began to laugh.

IV

◆ 17 ◆

Wired and Stoned

Reena said, "I love technology."

Sushama watched her as she typed on her laptop, her fingers flying.

"What are you doing?" Sushama asked, peering into the screen.

"Mom, you know what I am doing," Reena answered, fingers still flashing.

"These are pictures? Photos?" asked Sushama, looking at the page that had opened on the screen.

"Hmm," said Reena. "Of course, Mom, it is evident."

Sushama frowned. Kids had no patience with their parents when they became old. "I am asking only, *na*..." she said, "how will I know anything if I don't ask?"

"Valid point," Reena nodded, now smiling at her mother.

~

Someone had visited her website and said that merely posting pretty pictures of jewellery and giving them fancy names was not enough, customers wanted to know if they could afford the items. After all, in a restaurant, menu cards without prices did not work, did they?

So Reena was revamping the website, also giving quotes for bulk orders, adding prices for individual items, showing their availability, time needed for orders to be processed, cash on delivery, information regarding cancellation of orders.

"I like this piece," Sushama said, pointing to one. "Aren't you happy I encouraged your creativity?"

"Yes," Reena turned suddenly and grinned at her mother. "All I have learnt is from you, even the business *sutra*, Mom, you know, the essence of good business."

"But not technology *sutra*," Sushama grimaced.

"Well," said Reena, "that's one *sutra* or knowledge core you will have to let me teach you. Are you game?"

Sushma said, "What will I learn? I am not interested in tapping keys. Anyways, my fingers hurt."

"Mother, don't make excuses, you are being too tough on yourself. Once you get the hang of it, it's pretty simple."

"You go ahead and do your email, gmail, and I will go make some tea."

"Thanks, Mom, basil-flavoured please, and lighter than usual," said Reena. "That's just what I need in this soggy weather."

Outside, everything lay hidden by a curtain of rain. Above it, a grey, threatening sky heralded a heavy monsoon season.

"Okay then, I shall make some onion *pakodas* too."

"Yippee!" said Reena, and turned back to her computer screen.

It was so much easier to deal with customers in this fashion. She did not have to send flyers or go house to house for clients, things she had done when she had just begun her business. All the net-savvy people could be contacted to join her client list, and she was happy enough with that for the time being. She had recently started out on the online venture, and twenty-seven customers had already confirmed their orders. Ninety-one had sent queries. She had a long list of potential clients she planned to send emails to. As for the customers who had no access to the net, she would find a way to contact them too.

Reena smiled and looked again at the necklace her mother had admired. She liked the way the thin silver wires gleamed with the multi-coloured stones placed in-between. The necklace would look lovely on her mother.

Once in a while, she could place an order too. *No harm in that*, she thought.

"Here's one for you, Mother!" she said, and placed the order for a scintillating piece from 'Wired and Stoned'.

Sushama called out from the kitchen, "Ayub Khan, the carpenter, is on the phone regarding the chicken wire work, what should I tell him?"

"Tell him I'll call him," said Reena. She tried not to think of how the necklace looked like chicken wire, with beaded raindrops. "Beautiful, all the same," she murmured, and closed her laptop.

~

For the last week, Ayub Khan the carpenter was at large in Reena's home, making wood frames for the balcony, to which he would attach chicken wire, to keep the pigeons out. The pigeons were a menace, sitting on the washing line and shitting on the clothes hung out to dry.

He'd worked for Reena's parents when she was a child. Now, decades later, he still came and worked for her. He was old and eccentric but had not lost his physical prowess, nor his *jugaadpan*: the ability to find workable solutions.

However, he was set in certain ways.

The last time Ayub Khan had been over, Anand had wanted a precious painting hung on the drawing room wall. He advised Ayub Khan to use a drill machine and a rawl plug to make sure that the painting hung well and secure. Ayub Khan categorically told him that such a nail would shake free soon enough and the painting would surely fall. He did not want to be responsible for such damage.

Anand gave up. "I bow to your craftsmanship," he said.

So Ayub Khan had hammered a hole in the wall using a thick nail, then chipped away on a piece of wood to fashion a wooden *gutti* that he hammered into the hole, then put a nail through this *gutti*. From this secured nail, the painting would hang, never to fall. No plastic rawl plug could replace his wooden *gutti*, and no drill machine could replace his hammer and chisel.

Now he called out to Reena, "*Behenji...*"

Ayub Khan had made the frames and had stretched the chicken wire across them. He now had to place and fix the frames onto the iron railing and the concrete roof of the balcony.

"How will you do this?" asked Reena.

"Simply," he said, not batting an eyelid, "I will use a hammer drill."

"You will?" Reena raised her eyebrows. "Simply?"

"Just organize a double ladder for me, please."

That settled that, she thought, when her gaze fell on the table top he had finished laminating. It looked like a wounded soldier with white masking tape around the edges.

"This table..." Reena pointed at it.

"Yes, *behenji*? It is done."

"What happened to all the tiny nails you used to place all around the sides and turn in to keep the laminate in place?" Reena asked.

"Oh no, *behenji,* that is all old stuff. I put this tape, and after twenty-four hours, you remove it. Your laminate is all set. I don't need to come to remove the nails. This is fast and clean work."

"*Haan,*" Reena said, "I guess so."

"No guessing, I know *ji,*" he said. "*Humey pataa hai ji...* what this is... *technaalaji.*" He nodded vehemently. His hennaed hair was sprung orange wire, hitting a yellow, weathered face. He was wise and with technology.

Anand had been listening to them from behind his newspaper. He lifted his head now and smiled. "Your *behenji* also knows a lot about technology. She is always using her laptop, designing things."

◆ 18 ◆

The Greedy and the Innocent

Diwali would come around November, and then Christmas in December. Reena wanted to make some really funky jewellery sets for the festive season.

In the meantime, she was busy with some serious work, preparing jewellery designs for a wealthy family where the one and only daughter was getting married in November. The daughter, Namita Bajaj, wanted jewellery sets for six cousins and two friends. The sets were to be different, each to suit a young woman's looks, height, colouring and dress. It was a great order, a welcome order, but also one that required Reena's undivided attention.

The bell rang and she saw Harinmoy standing at the door. She said, "Come in, I think I need the tea more than you."

"Sir is not there?" he asked.

"Yes, how do you know?"

"I see it in your face, Madam, the loneliness," he said, and sat down. "So I have come at the right time for tea?"

"I am not lonely, Harinmoy," she said, "in fact, when he is away I get more work done..." and she pointed to her laptop.

He looked at the designs on her laptop while she brewed the tea in the kitchen. "Ah, interesting, Madam, this fascination for wire? You like twists and turns, is it not, dear?"

"Okay, SS," she said, coming back with the tea, "what about the coloured stones then, what do they mean to you?"

"A love for colour and a colourful life, but with the steadiness of stones, a certain grounding needed as well. These designs give a reading of you."

"Umm... huh... I love diamonds too, you know."

"Not really, that's just your need to be a part of the pack, despite knowing that you are different..."

He looked at the earrings in her ears. They were long silver loops of varied lengths attached to a slim hook, and a small blue stone hung in the centre of the loops. "Now, these earrings, they suit you."

"My latest find in some back-of-beyond place I went with Vandana," she said, touching them self-consciously. "Not expensive at all."

"Madam, not expensive, but close to your heart. See your work also, Madam, you love to do it. Everything is not about money."

"Money is important." Reena liked earning her own bucks and the independence it brought her.

"I don't bother so much about the money," he said. "I have found that what has to come to you will come, and what has to go, will go. So I have stopped caring, especially recently."

Reena looked at him, curious to know more.

"For the past year, I had joined a 'committee', where I was saving Rupees 4,000/- a month and it would make Rupees 48,000/- by the end of the year. I had managed to put the money together and had hoped to get a lump sum at the end. However, I came to know that the 'committee' man disappeared with the money just before he had to pay."

"*You* will never get it back? But you are a Super Sleuth! You just have to follow his trail."

"I am not paid for following his trail, and I do not earn so much, Reenaji. If I chase him, I will lose more time, energy, clients, and then he will be responsible for a loss of not just 48k, but of much more."

"Umph," Reena said, "of course."

"See, I called his son up a couple of times. The son kept reassuring me that the money would be given the next day, then the day after, then after fifteen days. I did not pursue it after that.

"It was my foolishness to put the money in something where there is no receipt, no proof, just the hope that I will get my lump sum and some more once the kitty opens in my name. I had hoped to get lucky, but I was actually being foolish."

He removed his hat now and placed it on the table. "So you see, even an SS like me, can be fooled."

"Anyone can... sometimes," said Reena.

"Anyone can; anyone who is greedy or innocent. I was both at the time. Yet, there are many people who do this, and nothing happens. Everything goes well. After all, that is why such a thing has survived."

Reena did not have the heart to tell him that such schemes survive because there is always some *bakra*, some goat willing to get his throat cut for a sacrifice. Of course he would know that. But maybe even sleuths, and smart ones at that, had their Achilles heel. Maybe he was not that smart about money.

He could earn lots more by doing what he did, yet he was not that geared towards it. Or it could be that, as he said, he had stopped thinking too much about it.

"Thank god tea is relatively cheap," she said. "We can afford it."

Harinmoy smiled, and she saw for the first time a dimple in his left cheek.

◆ 19 ◆

Family Matters

"There are some things you can't control," Harinmoy said, as he sat sipping his tea. "A relative of mine got into trouble with a woman; she accused him of showing her some... um... wrong... pictures, in order to have a... ahem... a... what to say... *good time*... with her. So she called the police.

"He was my relative, so I had to help him, even if I felt he deserved what he was getting. He said of course that he had done nothing of the sort; that she was just trying to frame him because he was not agreeing to leave his wife for her."

"Why did you help him?"

"Well, he is my relative, from my village, I have to. Family is very strong in the village, even the entire village is akin to family, and this is my Uncle, my mother's brother."

"So what did you do?"

"I had to pay the police Rupees 20,000/- to get him released from their clutches."

"Why did you pay?"

"He does not have money."

So you are not a millionaire either, thought Reena. She let it go, for there was no need to rub it in, he had already paid, in any case.

"Why? Your relative must be earning something?"

"He is an alcoholic. He is always at the club at Ghaziabad, boozing. He meets that woman friend also there."

"He is unmarried? He can marry her."

"No need, his wife and kids are in the village. The extended family takes care of them, and they do not know what he is doing here."

"So what the woman was saying was true?"

"The police believed her. They are always on the side of the woman nowadays."

"Which is a good thing, for women are always compromised," said Reena, vehemently.

"Madam, she is a 'more-than-good' friend. You think he will just be showing pictures to her... just like that..."

She pursed her lips. It was best to keep quiet.

"In any case, Madam, the point of the matter is that I paid Rupees 20,000/-, not knowing if and when I will get the money back."

Reena said, "You most probably will not, going by what I have just heard of him."

"Yes, Madam, I am not sure too, so I think, this money had to go, *na*?"

◆ 20 ◆

You Get What You Will

Harinmoy sat, empty teacup in hand, staring at the two yellow flowers on the blue cup. "More and more, Reenaji, I have come to believe, do what you will, what you can. But you will get what you deserve. That only."

Reena noticed that reminiscing about his life had made his eyes wide and sad. "Yikes, sounds pretty ominous," she said, trying to lighten his mood.

"Let us take food," he said. "Now, the food is on the plate. It is in front of you. Your wife has served you and is waiting for you to begin. The phone rings, something urgent has come up, and you tell your wife, 'I will just come back and eat.' But it is four to five hours before you return. In the meantime, she has given that food to someone else, maybe your son, or to the dog, who knows. That particular plate of food... you did not get to eat it."

"There is a saying, *'daane daane pe likha hai khane wale ka naam,'*" said Reena.

Harinmoy nodded. "Just my point, *on each morsel is written the name of the one who gets to eat it*," he said.

"So it is with all other things in life. So it is that I have stopped hankering after money or placing too much emphasis on collecting it or keeping it.

"There are clients who owe me money but I have not gone to collect it from them. If they need me again, they will call me, and then we will see."

"But that way you lose the money often," Reena gasped.

"As I said, I do not know if I have lost it or gained it; if it is to be mine, I will get it sometime."

He had looked like someone she could not even sit next to when they first met. And here she was talking to him and enjoying his company and all the stuff he talked. It had nothing to do with his being a detective and a sleuth, poking into other people's lives and making money from it.

"Harinmoy," said Reena, "this is the problem with us Indians, we are so fatalistic. We don't try. You should go after your money, it is hard-earned cash."

"Yes, but I also know that if I have to get it, I will, it is not running away."

"You have to give chase."

"Madam, I chase." He grinned. "But I do that to earn my money, and don't think it is all that much fun finding out what is happening where. It can get quite sleazy and sick."

"I understand. Under the surface, lives are messy."

"Now, take Prateeksha's case, for example. She is paying me to chase her husband. Do you think she will be happy knowing the end result? Or he will be happy to know that she is employing me to investigate his whereabouts, among other things? Either way, that relationship will take a lot to survive."

"So you think that your Uncle has a better relationship, with his wife unaware of what he is up to here?"

"Well, Uncle's wife is happy and trusting. Innocence has advantages."

Reena shook her head. Men had all the freedom to travel, inveigle others, play around, while women stayed at home, trusting, faithful, with kids and relatives to take care of.

Harinmoy read her mind.

"Don't think all women are the same, Reenaji. Now that lady friend of my Uncle's... she is not as simple as you take her to be. She ensnared my Uncle with her charms, and he used to buy her a lot of things when he was not spending on alcohol. But she wanted him to marry her and provide for her. He did not agree to that."

Reena sneered, "*Wah!* He is enjoying her company and what not here, with no commitments at all, and has a wife at home to boot. And no guilt pangs either, *wah.*"

"Madam, she is too, taking advantage of him."

Reena stopped herself. "Okay, Harin, forget it, you know I will always side with the woman."

"And I cannot take sides, I just know human nature is what it is, I have seen too much." He shook his head, closed his eyes and pursed his lips.

Reena could not help laughing at the picture he made. "Let me get you more tea," she said.

"Thank you Madam," he said, "you are very kind."

Not that much, she wanted to tell him, as she walked into the kitchen to make the tea, *I couldn't stand you in the beginning.*

She smiled as she made masala tea, the *dhaba* way. She poured a mixture of water and milk into the saucepan, brought it to a boil, put in the tea leaves and lowered the flame. She then dropped a couple of cardamom pods, a small stick of cinnamon and two cloves into this and allowed the concoction to cook and cook till it was thick and milky and fragrant with the smell of the spices. Then she strained it into the blue cup with the yellow flowers, added some cream on top, and sweetened it with two spoons of sugar.

For herself, no cream and no sugar, she was on a diet. Then she put in a half teaspoon of sugar. You take what you allow yourself to take, she whispered to herself, rolled her eyes, and walked into the drawing room with the two steaming cups.

"By the way, Madam," he said, "I am leaving now, chasing after Anirban Dasgupta. I shall return with him."

"Amen to that," she said. "But, where are you going chasing him?"

"I shall tell you, Madam," said Harinmoy.

21

Where is Anirban?

Harinmoy returned to speak with Reena a few days later.

Reena had just finished supervising the housework and her nerves were on edge. Parvati had to be given instructions all the time. One day she would forget to dust the study, another day she would forget to put the cups and saucers in their proper place.

Reena was glad to see him. With Harinmoy, she could forget about housework and its related hang-ups.

Dabbing her flushed face with her sari *pallu*, she invited him in.

His face gleaming with excitement, Harinmoy said, "Things are catching fire!"

"Oh, some new developments then, Harinmoy?"

"Madam, as you know, I make friends, I ask around."

"I know," said Reena. "You could write an Indian version of 'How to Make Friends and Influence People'."

"Joking, Madam? What is that?"

"No, seriously. It is a well-known book written by a famous American called Dale Carnegie."

"And what it has to do with me?"

"Well, you seem to instinctively know what he is talking about."

"Oh, Madam! A compliment you are giving, I think..."

"I think too," Reena smiled.

"Well, so coming back to something of great importance. I know where Mr Anirban Dasgupta most probably is."

"Oh! How did you find this out? Oh, let's have some tea," said Reena.

She dabbed her face once more with her sari *pallu*. She needed this break.

~

Harinmoy sipped his tea. He leaned back on the dining room chair and patted his stomach. "It was not easy. Finally, you won't believe it; I get the answer from Sanjay Singh."

"Our... Sanjay Singh?"

"Yes, your driver and what you call it... Man Friday, Madam."

"How did that happen? What does Sanjay know?"

"Well, I got the information through his friend, really."

"Okay."

"Yes. I am friendly with all the drivers, you know."

Reena knew that Harinmoy hobnobbed with the drivers, the maids, the *paan-waala,* the *chai-waala,* the *istri-waala*, the society guards, the labourers... He most probably smiled and said hello to the other ladies who lived in the apartment building. He had no problems talking to anyone. After all, he was talking to her as well, wasn't he? Having tea with her, wasn't he?

"Do you have tea with other ladies in the society here?"

"Oh, no, Madam, not even with Prateeksha! In you I have found a true friend who understands me."

Reena grinned. "A true SS like you?"

"That too, that too, Madam. When I talk with you, many things fall into place. With no one else can I share these very important details of the case, is it not, dear?"

"So, tell me, where is Anirban supposed to be?"

"Not so fast, Madam, this is no way to understand these things," said Harinmoy, smiling a little.

Reena picked up her teacup. There was not much tea left in it. She put the cup down and looked at Harinmoy.

"Okay," she said.

This man relished revealing things slowly, but it drove her nuts. Reena drummed her fingers on the table. She looked outside the window. She peered at the wall clock, whose hands seemed to have suddenly stopped.

Harinmoy sat quietly, his eyes closed, his hands clasped across his stomach.

Harinmoy opened his eyes. He unclasped his hands. Finally, he spoke.

"Anirban loves fish, he exists for eating fish. He has married stupid. No, wise according to others, but stupid for him. So how does he find the answer to the problem? He goes to his hometown. He can have his fill of fish there. There is where I'm going... to find him and get him back."

Reena looked at him, her eyes wide and her eyebrows raised. "Sanjay Singh told you this? But Sanjay Singh is from Punjab. How does he know anything about Anirban or his hometown?"

"Who told me this? I told you I got the information through Sanjay's friend. His friend is Bengali, his name is Bimal."

Harinmoy made a pyramid with his fingers and placed it under his chin, obviously enjoying himself. "I talk to him in his language, he reveals everything to me! He stays in same village as Anirban. He has a bone to pick with Anirban for Anirban does not see him, looks through him, though they are brothers, given they belong to the same village. So, he reveals all, tears in his eyes, holding on to my arm, sobbing over it.

"I allow him to do this, to sob over my arm, put his head on my shoulder and cry. I ask for the *thikana*, the address of the place. The man offers to take me to his village, to accompany me there. I have agreed. We leave tomorrow."

Harinmoy removed the pyramid of fingers from under his chin and leaned back once more. "Thank you for the tea, Madam, it gives me so much energy."

Reena looked at him, dazed. *Why would the man need extra energy? He was jumping from foot to foot and raring to go.*

"Best of luck, Harinmoy," she said, looking down into her teacup and smiling.

Talk about things catching fire.

~

A few days later, Anand asked Reena, "And where is Harinmoy? I haven't seen him around for a while?"

"Oh-ho. You are worried about the SS?"

"Well, someone has to be on his tail as well. He can't be the only one chasing after people."

"Well, he is in some village in Bengal."

"You mean... Anirban is in some Bengali village now? What's he doing there?"

"Most probably filling his stomach with fish."

"Yuck. That sounds gross, Reena."

"Okay. How about this? Most probably he is walking around a lake filled with fish, and singing a romantic song to some village belle. Does that sound better to you?"

"Reena, that sounds awful too. That poor girl, Prateeksha, crying for a man like him."

Reena said nothing. She, too, after all, hated to cook fish. Thank god Anand had other interests; fish was not among his major obsessions. She just hoped that Anirban returned soon so that Prateeksha stopped crying... on Anand's shoulder, for example.

Her mobile rang. "Yes?" she said. It was Harinmoy.

22

A Village called Chirulia

"Madam, can you help me please?" Harinmoy's voice crackled on the other end, low and distant.

"Of course, where are you, Harinmoy?"

"Madam, I am in a village called Chirulia, near Digha, three hours journey from Kolkata, oh... please could you call Prateeksha Madam to talk on your phone?"

"I'll go over and see if she is there, Harinmoy... hold on... or better, should I call you back?"

"No, no, it is important to speak now, I have Mr Anirban next to me and he has to talk to Prateeksha Madam... it is to do with his return..."

~

Reena stood in front of Prateeksha's door and rang the bell. She did not have to wait long thankfully and a rather preoccupied Prateeksha opened the door for her. "Oh, Auntie, sorry, I was not expecting anyone..." She wore a printed cotton dressing gown, and her hair was tied behind her neck in a loose, untidy knot.

"Call from Harinmoy..." said Reena and handed her the mobile.

Prateeksha said, "Oh... thanks, actually my mobile has been off... please sit..." she motioned towards the sofa in the hall. "Yes, Harinmoy... " she said into the phone, "Oh, so you have found him?"

"Excuse me, Auntie, I need to talk in private, please wait, though..." said Prateeksha, and walked into her bedroom with Reena's mobile.

Reena had no choice but to wait. She waited for about ten minutes, and then lost patience. Prateeksha could return the mobile when she was done with the call. She stood up and quietly shut the front door behind her, walked up to her apartment door, and rang the bell.

Anand opened the door for her. "Welcome home," he said. "No mobile, I see."

Reena nodded. "It's with her. Well, the bill is going to come to her."

"Pretty curious, this," said Anand. "She must have had her mobile off."

"Yes, something like that. We'll know soon enough what all this is about."

An hour later, the doorbell rang. Prateeksha was at the door. Her hair was combed and tied in a ponytail. She was dressed in a white *kurta* over blue jeans. She definitely looked more presentable than when Reena had last seen her.

"Thank you, Auntie," she said, handing the mobile to Reena. "Hello, Uncle," she said, looking at Anand.

"Come in and sit down, Prateeksha," said Anand, smiling at her.

"Thank you, Uncle. Both of you are so kind."

"Oh, welcome," said Anand, his eyes twinkling at her.

"Sorry, but I have to rush. I have a presentation to prepare, and that is why I had taken leave and luckily was at home, otherwise I would have not been able to talk to Harinmoy."

"Everything okay?" asked Anand.

"Oh yes, quite a relief that Anirban has been located, at some god-forsaken place called Chirulia, near Digha.

Seems it is his home town or village or whatever. Imagine how little one knows about the other person in an arranged marriage. I have not even heard of these places."

"Where are you from then?" asked Reena.

"Oh, Auntie, you know, though I am a Delhi girl, I have studied in Simla and worked in Mumbai, so I guess Anirban's background is quite different from mine."

Reena thought of Bimal the driver, from the same village as Anirban, from Chirulia, in fact.

"Yet you are together now, for better or for worse," said Reena.

Anand's eyebrows shot up in surprise.

Prateeksha sighed and stood up. "Thanks Auntie, thanks Uncle, you must excuse me. I am just glad that Anirban will soon return. I just want him back..."

Reena stared after her as Anand walked her to the door. The girl had almost convinced her that she really wanted her husband back. But then, why was her mobile switched off? Should she not have been waiting for a call from her husband?

V

◆ 23 ◆

The Return of Harinmoy

Harinmoy had returned and sat himself down on the other side of the dining table. The dining table was Reena's multi-purpose work-station. She designed her jewellery on the dining table, used her laptop on it, cut vegetables on it, served tea on it and entertained the likes of Harinmoy here as well.

He smiled as he looked at her laptop, the scattered papers and sketch pens, and at her, sitting opposite him, spectacles perched on her nose. "You know, Madam, I can only get the kind of tea I want at your place, made by you," he said.

Reena smiled, her eyes crinkling with pleasure. "Thank you, Harin," she said, feeling special.

Harinmoy said, "There is much that has happened with Prateeksha Madam. I shall give you an update."

Reena already knew that Anirban Dasgupta, her next door neighbour, had come home. However, from the look of things, Prateeksha was still not happy. Harinmoy was still on her payroll, so obviously there were other things to be settled.

Recently, there had been scenes in Flat No. 69. Prateeksha was heard throwing tantrums, shouting and storming out of the house in anger. However much

Reena had wanted to ignore all this, she could not help but hear it all.

Harinmoy took a long sip from the blue cup with two yellow daisies painted on it, and said, "This should have a butterfly on the flowers, is it not, dear?"

Reena said, "I think it would be a case of overcrowding, then..."

"Oh, Madam SS, you have done it again, one flower and one butterfly, is it not, dear?"

Reena wondered when she could tell him, very politely, to leave the 'dear' out of his conversation.

"The two flowers look pretty enough..." said Reena.

"Prateeksha, she is as pretty as a flower herself," said Harinmoy, "but she thinks her husband does not love her and has gone off chasing some other woman."

"But there is another woman in their house, isn't there? He has brought her back with him." Reena had caught a glimpse of a young girl in a *sari*. A beautiful Bengali girl with a long black plait down her back and big, fish-shaped eyes outlined with kohl.

The girl had disappeared inside the house, but Reena knew she stayed there. She had seen *saris* drying on the washing line and she had never seen Prateeksha wear one.

Harinmoy said, "Yes, Reena Madam. I had to persuade him a lot before he agreed to return. But he set his own terms. He brought a woman back with him to cook the fish which he would surely eat."

Reena *tch-tched*. "My god. Poor Prateeksha."

"No, no, Madam, it is not as you think. He has just got this woman who knows how to cook fish the way he wants it. That is what he had told Prateeksha too, on the phone when he spoke with her before he returned with me, and she had reluctantly agreed. You remember I had called your number?"

"How can I forget, Harinmoy? I had to walk to her flat and give her my mobile. She had her mobile switched off? Why?"

"She did not want to take his calls. Moreover, she has been working on some project lately, and did not want to be disturbed. That is what she said to me. Anyway, thanks to you, I could connect the two of them on the phone."

"Prateeksha agreed to the woman coming to stay and to the fish cooking and all of this... the smell, the bones, and what have you?" Reena had put up with the smell of fish cooking next door ever since this new woman, brought to cook for Anirban, had moved in. She hated the smell of fish.

Harinmoy continued, "So you see, it is all very fishy, Reenaji, he is a fishy type."

"I bet Prateeksha thinks so too," she said.

"Ha ha," he laughed. "But, you know, it is these small things which become the big thing."

"Hmm," said Reena. "Some more tea?"

"Madam," he said, "thank you..."

Reena poured more tea for him from the kettle she had prepared before. The tea was hot and flavoured and the smell of cardamom filled the air.

"Aah..." he murmured in appreciation; then continued. "See, Prateeksha's husband, the good Mr Anirban Dasgupta, as we know, loves fish. He needs to have fish every day.

"And Prateeksha, she doesn't know or care about fish. She is vegetarian, the *pucca* vegetarian type." Harinmoy squirmed as he said it, as if he could not understand how anyone could subsist on pure vegetarian meals.

He said, "So I asked Prateeksha Madam why she was not happy, now that her husband had returned. I had hunted him out in this village in Bengal where he said he spent his childhood and he brought back this girl from there. He says she is the daughter of his childhood cook, though looking at her you would not know it."

"Yes, they are educated and smart nowadays, why should they remain cooks?" said Reena.

"Well, he went there to actually look for his old cook, Mishima. But Mishima was dead. Instead, he found this girl, Sharmila, Mishima's daughter, still living near their old house in the village.

"Sharmila cooked fish for him as a welcome, and he was bowled over. He said he had gone there for a while, just wanting to get away from Delhi, the metropolitan city, and be among his people."

"What about Prateeksha? He forgot all about her?" asked Reena.

"After eating all that fish and finding someone willing to cook it, he had forgotten all his anger at Prateeksha. He told me he tried calling her but she was not taking his calls. I checked with Prateeksha and she finally agreed that she had ignored his calls."

"Oh!"

"Well, what do I care if I am sent on a chase that could have been avoided? I got the money for it, she has paid me." He leaned back in the chair. "And Madam, I can tell you I am glad I went. Digha is a beautiful place. I had quite an experience. Let me tell you about it..."

~

"I reached Kolkata with Bimal. We had taken a train to get there from Delhi. Then we took a bus from Kolkata to Digha. It was a three hour journey. I am used to travel, Madam, so I was not so tired. Nor was Bimal, used as he is to the hard life. And then when I saw Digha, I forgot whatever pains and aches the travel had given me. It is a beautiful city near the sea. I had not expected it to be like this. But we did not stop there. We had to travel another 40 km before we reached Chirulia, the village that Mr Dasgupta comes from.

"When we reached Chirulia, Bimal was beside himself with joy. He jumped off the bus holding on to my hand, and I just saved myself from a major fall. I steadied myself and dusted my pants. Bimal walked jauntily on and asked me to follow him, which I did, much like an obedient dog.

"After a while he stopped near a hut and said he was home. He pointed at the distance. I had to just walk a few yards more and I would come to Anirban's house. That was all.

"So, I began to walk. I saw Anirban's home. It was an old building, falling apart.

"But nearby was a hut. I could smell the fish cooking. Anirban had to be here. I walked into the hut, a bit unsure, but what a sight I saw.

"It was a mud hut, with a low asbestos roof. I saw the fish, wrapped in green leaves, cooking on a mud *chulah*. The smell was overwhelming, I stood there mesmerized. A woman sat near the *chulah*, on her haunches, her *sari* drawn up to her knees, she was young... and beautiful.

"I walked in and saw this. No wonder the man did not want to move from there. He has money. He wants comfort and relaxation, and he has some childhood memories to relive. He does that here in Chirulia.

"I can understand him not wanting to leave that place. Prateeksha and Delhi would be foreign to him, strange to this life. I cannot forget the smell of that fish. My mouth waters as I think of it."

Reena thought to herself, *It is not just the fish.*

She said, "So there is the woman, right?"

"There is, and there isn't. She is an extension of a childhood memory for him... he just likes her cooking. It reminds him of his cook, Mishima; he was brought up on her food. Mishima cooked for them all her life till his parents died. Anirban, of course, had left home a long time back, to study outside."

"He must have known of this daughter though?" Reena said, suspicion colouring her voice.

"Madam, you are too much SS! I do not think he had any idea about Mishima's family life. She was just his cook."

He sat back and sighed. "They were both shocked to see me there. Then of course, I shared the fish with them. I had the most satisfying meal.

"We walked outside the hut and talked. Anirban did realize that his holiday was over. But he was going to return on his own terms. As you can see, it has happened."

Reena sat there, taking it all in. So much drama! It was bound to happen in the lives of those who came to stay in Flat No. 69. This was surely the end to their turbulent story?

Harinmoy said, "By the look of things, Prateeksha is happy to have her husband home, and Anirban is also happy to have his wife in his arms and the fish in his food."

He stood up, flicked his wrist and glanced at his gold-plated watch.

"Got to go, Madam, it is getting late. Thank you for the tea."

• 24 •

A Case to Crack

A few days later, Harinmoy was back at Reena's home.

Reena had just sent off an order, and was very satisfied. The order was for a set of pearl mesh earrings, a pearl mesh square pendant necklace, and a pearl mesh cuff for the wrist. Within a fine border of sterling silver encrusted with tiny zircons was wrought a spider web of silver wire which held within it a small glowing pearl. The jewellery was light, contemporary and elegant, and had become an instant hit online. Reena had priced the set slightly higher to lend it a certain exclusivity, and her gambit had worked.

She sat back and put her feet up. She looked at her feet. She really needed a pedicure. *Time to call Anjali again*, she thought.

Reena glanced at Harinmoy. He sat opposite her, nodding his head in dismay.

"Why so worried, Harinmoy?"

"Though her husband is back, Prateeksha is still not happy. Madam, the crux of the matter remains the same. The cause of the dispute continues to be FISH. Fish is there in the house, isn't it?"

"So it is. In fact, I can sniff it in the air all the time now. Oh, let me brew some tea, Harinmoy."

"Yes, Madam, that would be a relief, to have some tea."

~

Harinmoy put his teacup down and wiped his mouth with his red handkerchief. He then pushed it into his blue pants pocket. These were not blue jeans, they were blue cotton pants; the kind kids wear to school.

"I thought the crux of the matter had become Sharmila... his disappearing, and returning with her..."

"No, Madam, Sharmilas may come and go, but Anirban needs his fish."

"Oh," said Reena. "So let Sharmila stay and cook the fish. Everyone is happy."

"No. Sharmila also makes Prateeksha unhappy. Prateeksha thinks Sharmila has her eyes on Anirban."

"So let Anirban and his fish and Sharmila go."

"Is it so easy, Madam?" He gave her a quizzical look. "Prateeksha loves her husband."

Harinmoy put his black patent leather gloves on the table. He zipped and unzipped his bright yellow jacket. Reena wished he would stop; it was giving her a headache.

He gave his jacket a final zip up. "In such a situation, any moment, she will burst into tears, is it not, dear?'"

"So why does she not cook him fish the way he wants it, if she loves him so much?" Reena asked.

"Simple question. No simple answer." He paused, pursed his lips, sucked in his breath. *He looks quite like a fish himself*, thought Reena.

"Madam, I had this conversation with her the other day. Let me tell you about it.

H: 'Prateeksha Madam, why not cook him fish.

Way to a man's heart is through his stomach.
An old rule but it works…'

P: 'I hate fish, can't stand it.'

H: 'Okay, then why did you marry him?'

P: 'Arranged marriage.'

H: 'Arranged? But he is not from your caste.'

P: 'I know that. He is also a Bengali, I am not.'

H: 'A match made in heaven?'

"I saw the look on her face and relented, Reenaji. I was naturally curious now. This is what Prateeksha told me, her eyes swimming with tears."

> P: 'I had a great job and was earning very well.
> I kept refusing the marriage offers much to
> my parents' chagrin, and at 27 they told me
> I would be soon over the hill as far as the
> marriage market was concerned. I could not
> care, but then my parents did. The guys I saw
> from my community just did not measure up.
> So they widened their net, so to speak, and
> they found Anirban. He was good looking,
> polite, well-settled, and wanted to marry me.
>
> 'I was quite happy with the idea of settling
> down with him, before he said that he
> loved fish. I told him I was vegetarian. He said
> it was fine as long as I did not mind cooking
> fish for him. I thought, maybe he eats it once
> a month. I thought, maybe he will be so in

love with me that he will forget fish and maybe he will turn completely vegetarian.

'I did not know he ate fish every day! And I hate fish, it is so smelly a food. Yuck, how does he stomach it!'

Harinmoy continued, "Reenaji, this is how the whole thing unraveled some more."

H: 'So then be happy he has a cook.'

P: 'Now I have to live with fish and a fishwoman. I want them out, out of my life.'

Harinmoy said, "Madam, she made no bones about her views. I told her that if they don't go, you leave and go. But she burst into tears then.

"She said, 'How can I? I LOVE him. He has the most soulful eyes and he recites Bengali poetry in the most beautiful voice. No one in my parents' house even knows what poetry is. He sings to me.'"

Harinmoy looked at Reena. "It was so touching, so romantic. I found that I could not let matters be. The problem needs a solution. I have to think about it."

Reena sighed. She hoped the rectangle of Anirban, Sharmila, Prateeksha and the Fish soon sorted itself out. Her sketch pad and pen lay next to her laptop. She pulled these towards her and made a quick drawing of a rectangle, labeled the points, and drew a line through, cutting it so that Anirban and Prateeksha were on one side, and Sharmila and the Fish on the other.

She handed the sketch to Harinmoy.

His eyes popped. "Madam, you are true SS."

"Just don't give me the Hitler salute," she said, "I will faint on the spot."

"What, Madam?"

"Nothing, got to fly tomorrow to Hyderabad, so brain's a bit scrambled."

"And mine is fried, haha, joke is it not, dear?" he looked at her. "I shall leave you, Madam, have a safe journey. You will return to a cracked egg... case, I mean."

• 25 •

Expressways and Fartiquette

Namita Bajaj's parents had placed the order for jewellery with 'Wired and Stoned', on Namita's insistence. She did not want something traditional for her close friends and cousins.

She wanted something aesthetic and modern and light. Reena had the eight jewellery sets ready, and was now flying to Hyderabad to deliver them to Namita in time for her wedding, which was to take place three days later. Reena, who had been invited to all the wedding functions, had agreed to attend the *sangeet* before her return to Delhi.

This was important for her, for she knew that her designs, worn and displayed by the young girls at Namita's wedding, could be her ticket to more orders from such clients. Sitting in the cab taking her to T1 at the Delhi airport, from where she would catch her Indigo flight, she drummed nervous fingers on the door handle.

The cab was travelling too fast. The cab driver was talkative.

"You know, *Maddamji*," he said, "on the Delhi–Agra Expressway, four accidents happened two nights ago... you must have read in the papers?"

He paused and looked at her through the rear-view mirror. When Reena did not respond, he continued with his talk.

"*Maddamji*, forty cars crashed... at 10pm, 10.40pm, 11pm and 11.15pm!"

It was a winter morning, there was fog ahead, the cab was speeding and the man was talking about accidents.

Reena stuffed her hands into the pockets of her sweater, trying to understand the psychology of people like the cab driver.

It was as if by talking about things that had happened, mainly accidents, the danger of such things happening to you, in a similar situation, was warded off. Why else would the cab driver, a plump, young Sardar, talk about this while driving to the airport?

"The expressway is made of cement; fast cars often burst their tyres there. It will take some time before the expressway wears down and the cars don't experience this," he said.

Reena closed her eyes and saw dented cars, shattered glass, broken bodies and shouting, screaming drivers. She shivered and opened her eyes.

The young Sardar was smiling and driving merrily. He spoke as though he was describing his sister's wedding instead of the accidents he had read about.

"In the first accident, the tyre of an Innova punctured, and it parked on the side of the road. A couple of cars banged into that. They were driving at the speed of 150. The maximum speed allowed is 100 at the expressway, you know, *Maddamji*. So at that speed, coupled with the fog, they could see nothing, control nothing.

"In the second case, a truck dislodged a sack of red chillies on the road. To avoid this, the car following it braked, and there were ten cars behind this car. All the cars, *total ho gai si*. Of course, not only the cars, some people were also hurt.

"Two more accidents of a similar nature, *Maddamji*. In this way, four accidents and forty cars gone. Just on one foggy night on the expressway."

Reena looked out of the window. "Please," she said, "I don't want to hear all this."

"Okay, *Maddamji*." He paused for effect. "But you know, I can do it too, drive fast on the expressway. I have done the Delhi-Agra run in one and a half hours!" There was pride in his voice.

Reena was grateful when they had arrived at the airport and she was still in one piece.

She thanked him, paid him, and made her way inside the terminal. Soon, she messaged Anand that she was in her seat and the plane would take off in ten minutes.

There was a slight noise ahead of her and she looked up.

In one of the overhead luggage racks, someone's chewing gum had melted. It had stuck itself on all the suitcases. The air hostess and then the individual suitcase owners had begun to take turns to remove the sticky chewing gum which had spread itself along the length of the rack when the air hostess had pulled a suitcase out.

A peculiar thing to happen, thought Reena. She watched as the suitcase owners rubbed the white chewing gum off their suitcases. The air hostess had a crestfallen and apologetic look.

Someone behind her seat began to shake his leg, so Reena's seat also began to shake. On the seat beside the seat next to her, a large, bearded man had begun to snore, having fallen asleep even though the flight had yet to take off.

Reena turned to the young man behind her and said, "Please stop shaking my seat."

Two kids in the front began to shout, "Where are we going? Where are we going? To Hyderabad? Where in

Hyderabad, Mom?" Their mother, standing in the aisle to put the suitcases in the overhead luggage compartment, bent over to shush them. And farted loudly.

The kids put their fingers on their mouths and giggled. Their mother looked around, embarrassed, but no one had noticed it, except Reena, who looked down at her lap, pretending she had not heard anything.

Reena pulled out a magazine from her bag and hid her face behind it, giggling at her own fart experiences.

She knew for a fact that whenever she laughed loudly nowadays, she farted as well. It was something her daughter, Vandana, had pointed out to her.

~

One evening, Vandana had returned from work early, smiling and happy. She said she had finished her work in time, with no work-at-home overload.

Anand was also there, smoking a cigarette and reading a book.

Vandana cracked some joke and Reena, breaking out in peals of laughter, had released a few farts.

Vandana could not let the farts be. "Mom always has to fart. You can see how much she is enjoying the joke by the extent of the fart. And the louder the fart, the happier she is."

Then suddenly, Vandana broke into some kind of a stage act.

"Let's imagine your courtship days," she said.

"'Hey Reena, I want to marry you,' that's what you say, Dad," she said, looking at Anand.

"And Mom goes, 'Yes, Yes! I am so happy.' And she is frrr, frrr.....rrr farting away."

Reena and Anand burst out laughing. As she laughed, Reena farted some more. "Oh, Vandy, not fair," she hiccupped, clutching her hand to her chest, "this only happens nowadays, you know."

The scene made her smile as she thought of it. Reena put the magazine back into her bag. She fastened her seat belt, for they were ready for take-off. The boys in front were belted into their seats and were quiet. The bearded man continued to snore.

Reena closed her eyes and thought of the jewellery sets with her. She blew them a quiet kiss. They were ready for take-off too.

~

The next morning, Reena met the young and vivacious Namita at her posh office in Jubilee Hills. Namita had arrived there especially to meet Reena, away from the noise and action of the wedding preparations at home.

Namita's eyes sparkled on seeing the jewellery, and she gave Reena a quick, unexpected hug.

"Thank you," said Namita. "I am happy that you will be here for the *sangeet* tomorrow. Please keep the car for the day. You may want to sight-see. I hope the place you are staying at is fine?"

Reena nodded, too overcome. The cheque in her hand, she made her way out, ready to explore Hyderabad.

But first, she would call Anand and give him the good news!

❖ 26 ❖

The Bajaj Wedding Sangeet

Reena had been invited to the Bajaj wedding. She was, however, only attending the *sangeet*, a pre-wedding ceremony.

At the *sangeet*, songs are sung by the ladies. One of them plays the *dholak* and also sings. Another taps the *dholak* with a spoon, to keep a constant beat, to which everyone claps. Someone gets up and dances.

Old ladies and young girls, everyone feels the beat and the joy of celebration. The songs are loud, raunchy and merry, and aimed at reducing the pain of parting which the daughter feels on leaving the home of her parents.

As Reena stepped out of the car that had been sent for her that evening, Namita's mother, Priya Bajaj, met her at the door of their home. She smiled. "So glad you came, do come inside," she said. "We will have a more stylized *sangeet* event later in the evening. This one is for the close family members. We would like to consider you one."

Reena could see the warmth and softness in her eyes, and she smiled back.

Reena took in the splendour of the Bajaj home, decorated for their daughter's wedding. Little lights strung on the trees and hedges twinkled along the path.

Decorations in traditional motifs created a border on both sides of the path.

Beautifully dressed girls and boys welcomed the guests at the door. The boys wore embroidered *sherwanis* of ivory coloured silk, with *churidars*; the girls richly embroidered, multi-coloured *ghagra-cholis*, teamed with gold-coloured *dupattas*.

People were gently escorted inside, through the hall blazing with lights from overhead chandeliers. There was the smell of sandalwood in the air. Wide earthen bowls, filled with floating rose petals, lined the walls.

Reena, dressed in a turquoise blue *ghagra-kameez*, glittering with silver sequins, was happy she had managed to shed a few kilos before coming for the wedding.

She settled down on the carpeted floor, sitting next to the lady playing the *dholak*. Soon she was lost in the singing and merriment. The older generation was enjoying the songs, knowing the lyrics and feeling the tease behind the words.

The youngsters clapped and smiled and tried to mouth the unfamiliar words. The songs were rustic, with a spattering of words unfamiliar to the younger, more Westernized urban tongue. The songs reminded Reena of her childhood, when these gatherings were simpler.

She once again lost herself in the clapping and the beat as one by one the ladies stood up and danced.

So did some of Namita's cousins. Two of them wore the jewellery Reena had designed for them to wear at the wedding. They looked lovely. Reena smiled. Her designs did look good on these young women, enhancing their features and colouring. The girl with the sharp features and fair skin wore a turquoise and silver necklace. The silver had been intricately worked around the stones to make them look like raindrops, and she wore earrings to match. The plumper girl with softer features wore peacock-shaped earrings in red and gold. They went well with the *zari* work on her yellow *lehenga*.

Reena saw the women throw admiring glances at the jewellery and sensed she would receive more orders soon.

The girls pulled Namita up to dance with them, and she did so, grinning and giggling as she swung her slim hips to the song.

Namita's fiancé stood to the side with some of his friends, smiling sheepishly. He was invited to dance once. He gamely agreed, grinning as he jerked his arms and legs for a while, obviously not used to dancing to such songs.

Occasionally, a lady stood up with a fifty or a hundred Rupee note, waved it around the head of the dancer whose dance she was particularly impressed by, and handed it over to the person who was collecting the money.

When Namita danced, or her fiancé did, of course, several women stood up and circled the notes over their heads before dropping them into the lap of the collection lady.

The lady sitting next to Reena, one of Namita's aunts, turned to Reena and introduced herself as Vimla Maheshwari, of the Maheshwari Paper Mills. She was Mr Yogeshwar Bajaj's elder sister.

"I live nearby, also in this same posh locality of Jubilee Hills."

Reena was taken aback by this introduction. *Was she expected to be impressed?*

"I'm Reena Rajan, from Delhi," said Reena.

"The jewellery designer? How nice. I never needed to work, somehow."

Reena kept her cool. She did not have to explain her reasons to anyone.

"The arrangements are excellent," Reena said, by way of conversation. After all, this was Namita's aunt.

"Yes, there are certain advantages to having a girl child," said Vimla.

Reena looked at her with new respect. She was glad that this lady shared her views regarding girls. "Girls are a blessing, aren't they?" she asked, thinking of her own daughter, Vandana.

"Oh, how many daughters do you have?" Vimla was suddenly curious.

"One."

"Oh, no sons?" Vimla's voice held disappointment.

"Um, yes, one son as well."

Vimla smiled. "Balance *ho gaya*. No gain but no loss either," she said.

Reena looked away; she had heard such talk before. How girls were losses and boys were gains. The whole Indian social psychology teetered on this view. She had her own views, but she was not willing to hold forth today, not here, not now.

"I have three sons," Vimla said.

"You must really want a daughter," said Reena.

"Yes," said Vimla, "a daughter gives you a chance to show the world how well-off you are. You can show-off by spending on her marriage."

The singing grew louder, and Reena leaned in close to hear Vimla speak. "I... um... sorry, what did you say?"

"I said my brother can let the world know his worth because he has a daughter."

"Oh." Reena pursed her lips. She shifted on her bottom to move away, as if a gap could create enough distance between her and Vimla.

Her mind was trying to process what she had just heard and she found that it could not. Reena stood up to leave.

A hand pulled her into the centre, and instead of leaving, she found she was dancing to a song with one of Namita's young friends.

"C'mon Auntie, let's see your *dilli ka jhatka*," said the girl. The spoon picked up speed on the *dholak,* the clapping intensified to fill the room, and Reena danced.

As someone stood up and circled a note around her head while Reena whirled, she thought of her daughter. Vandana would have put Mrs Vimla Maheshwari firmly in her place.

Triple Whammy Plus One

Reena sat, dressed in her black embroidered Chanderi sari, with its fine red and gold border, at The Blue Fog in Vasant Kunj. At the suggestion of Amit and Vandana, Reena and Anand had come here to celebrate the success of her first big order, for the Namita Bajaj wedding.

The place was abuzz with people, but they were mostly *young*. She removed her shawl and placed it on the empty chair beside her. Nursing her drink, she smiled wanly at Anand, who seemed to be more attuned to the youthful ambience of the place.

I.

"Minnisha! It is Minnisha, omigod, after so many days... years, oh!" The woman tip-tapped towards Reena in her high heels, tripping along with excitement.

Though Reena was thankful to see that someone her age did visit the place, the rather well-preserved woman looked like no one she knew.

Reena smiled and said, "Uh, sorry, I am not..."

"Minnisha, don't tell me you don't remember, Loreto Convent, then Symbiosis... are you practising?"

The art of trying to know you at the moment, thought Reena drily, *that's what I am practising.*

"Sorry, I am not Minnisha. My name is Reena," she said, loud enough above the music and the woman's gushing.

"Really?" She looked aghast. "I could have sworn..."

"Must be my doppelganger."

Anand looked on, smiling.

"Pleased to meet you though, Ms...?" said Reena, breaking into a smile.

"Mrs Bhatia, Saroja Bhatia, Tamilian married to Punjabi you know..."

"Oh." Reena looked at her dark eyes with their even darker eyelashes.

"My husband is in the States. I am here for a friend. I am a lawyer, you see," she explained, catching her breath.

Reena did not see but she could guess.

"So your friend is with you?"

"Yes, there he is... I better join him now, okay, good meeting you, here is my card, if you need a lawyer, just call... I'm here for good now, Reena and..." she looked questioningly towards Anand now.

"Anand... Anand Rajan..."

"Anand, hi... Reena, do keep in touch... tada..."

She trotted off in the direction of the guy waiting for her.

2.

When she came out of the 'Ladies', Reena looked around for the soap dispenser.

"Here you are, love," said someone with a very Brit accent. She handed Reena a hand-sanitizer. Reena looked at her, dark and attractive, about twenty-five. If it was not for her British accent, Reena would have mistaken her for an Indian.

"Thank you," Reena said, and poured some onto her palm. She gave the sanitizer back to the woman.

"Oh, you can keep it, love."

Reena was surprised. "Thank you," she said again, "but I don't need it."

"Oh, yes, you can keep my passport too, if you like. You know, just keep anything you want."

She fluttered her hands in the air. "I so love Indians and India. I have applied for a job with the newspaper here. I studied journalism at Columbia. I hope I get it, I want to stay in India..."

"You are not Indian?"

"No, love, not Indian. Born in London, been there all my life, apart from that study stint in the US. I hate London so, want to stay in India... I love Delhi and Jaipur and Agra and Varanasi. So, you can keep anything... my passport too."

Reena stared. What was with this woman and her passport? She was drunk, perhaps? Well, almost everyone in The Blue Fog would be, it was that kind of a watering hole.

"I'm sure you will get the job," Reena said, rearranging the folds of her *sari*.

"Oh, thank you. Oh, keep it, love, keep it," said the woman, placing the sanitizer back in Reena's hand. She walked out, her curls flying out behind her.

We-ell. Reena stared at herself in the full-length mirror. She put the sanitizer in her bag and walked out into the courtyard. The night was turning out to be weirdly interesting.

Anand was nursing his single malt back at their table. "Your nose seems to have grown longer," he quipped.

"Hmm. I did take a long time powdering it," she smiled. She was more relaxed, feeling the vodka buzz now. "Wondering whether I should have another..."

"Why not, the night is young yet," said Anand.

"*Haan,* that's true. Might as well." She picked up the menu card. Her eyes scanned the glossy folder. She ran her hand over it. She loved the smooth *chikna* feel of it.

She signaled to the waiter. "*Sex on the Beach* for me."

The young man grinned. "Yes, Ma'am. And also something to eat?"

Anand said, "A couple of chicken steaks, rare for me and well-done for the lady. Sounds good, Reena?"

Reena nodded, smiling. She had to eat something so as to not feel very sleepy and high.

She hoped the kids would call it a night soon. Otherwise, she would call them and let them know that she and Anand were heading home. Reena could not take these late nights much anymore.

She downed the last of her drink. "How soon do you want to leave, Anand?" she asked.

"We can leave whenever you like," he said. "You are looking tired."

3.

With all the drinking she had done, Reena had to visit the loo again.

In the loo, she found a woman struggling with her dress, unable to zip it up fully. So Reena offered to lend a hand.

"Suck in your stomach a bit," said Reena, and zipped her up. "There you go."

"Thanks," said the woman. Reena looked at her closely now.

She had looked young to Reena at a distance, slim, high-heeled, off-the-shoulder dress and short-cropped hair, with highlights. Reena could now see the tiredness in the eyes, the slight droop to an otherwise perfectly made-up mouth. Touching fifty, was Reena's guess.

"I'm Kalpana," she said.

"Hi, Kalpana," said Reena, "got to use the loo."

~

When Reena stepped out, the woman was still there, combing her hair. "Do I look my age?" she asked, looking at Reena in the mirror.

"You look good," said Reena, "Hey, I'm done."

"Oh, yes, me too," said Kalpana, following her. A young man was standing a little away, smoking. Kalpana waved at him. Reena noticed his fine features, tanned skin and lean body. His hair was spiked and he had diamond studs in both ears.

"That's my boyfriend," whispered Kalpana. "Do you think I am cradle-snatching?" She looked at Reena, waiting for an answer.

"Do you think you are?" asked Reena.

"No, but he is so young."

"That's just fine."

"You think so?"

"All fair in love and war, darling," said Reena.

"Oh, thank you." Kalpana kissed Reena suddenly on both her cheeks and high-heeled fast towards her boyfriend. Reeling, from the kisses and the sudden impact of a woman's body against hers, Reena put her hand on the wall to steady herself.

Plus One

"Ma'am, you okay?" asked someone.

She looked at a young man, handsome and alone, looking at her with narrowed eyes.

"Oh ye-es," she said, one hand still on the wall.

"Let me help you inside, to your table."

"No, thanks," she snapped. "I can make it on my own."

"There's a light in your eyes, lady, something difficult to place. You sure?"

That's a new line, Reena thought. "Of course," she said.

He turned towards a young girl, in a powder-pink dress, walking up to him. "Hi, Sonali," he said to her. "You're kinda late, aren't you? Just a moment..."

He turned towards Reena again, who had dropped her hand from the wall and steadied herself on her heels. "Take care, lady in *sari*... with eyes of light."

'Eyes of light?' First time she had heard something like this.

Reena meandered carefully through the back door into the main restaurant area, headed towards her table and sank thankfully into her seat.

"Another drink, Anand," she said, "don't want to leave right now. Is that okay with you?"

Anand grinned. "Sure, the loo a particularly attractive place tonight?" He signaled for the waiter and Reena leaned back, kicking off her heels.

She said, "You can meet some interesting women there."

"Now spend some time with this interesting man, before you go again," he said.

"I'm not asking for it. I think it's something in the air tonight."

"Something about *you*, lady..."

She smiled then. Something about her, indeed. A lady in a *sari*... with eyes of light.

"Anand," she said, "about my eyes... do you think..." and blushed as he put his hand out to caress her fingers.

VI

◆ 28 ◆

A Matter of Perspective

Reena reclined on the sofa, her feet stretched out in front of her on a chair, catching up on her reading. Parvati had finished the mopping and dusting early and left. Anand was fast asleep in the bedroom, jet-lagged from another business trip. There was peace and quiet at home.

Reena placed her open book on her stomach and closed her eyes.

The doorbell rang and jolted Reena out of her near-slumber. *Who could it be at 4 in the afternoon?* she thought. She walked slowly to the door. Luckily, her legs were not paining today; the rest had done her good.

Harinmoy stood at the door, hat in hand. He removed his goggles and stepped in. "Ah, I seem to have disturbed your siesta?" he said, looking around.

Reena smiled. "Yes, looks like it, but as if that has ever bothered you..."

"Oh no, Reenaji! I know that you are usually working at this time, busy with your designs, so... please, don't say this... but, if you like, I should come another time? Though, you know, I have news..."

"No problem, Harin, I am wide awake, especially now that you say that you have news. However, Anand is sleeping inside, so we have to talk quietly."

He put his hat and goggles on the table. "We shall sit here, at our usual place?"

"Yes," grinned Reena, "and have our usual drink too."

Harinmoy said, "There air is a bit cold outside, but the room is warm."

He removed his shiny yellow jacket and sat down. He wore a green cotton shirt with big black polka dots. Around his throat was wound a striped silk scarf of rainbow colours. His clothes were, as usual, bright and badly-matched.

His white shoes with their brass buckles gleamed.

Reena closed her eyes for a moment and then opened them. "I'll make some tea," she said, and made a beeline for the kitchen.

~

Harinmoy looked at her conspiratorially over the teacup. "Sniff the air, Reenaji, do you smell fish?"

"No... oo..." She had not smelled the fish smell for some time now. Otherwise, whenever she stepped onto her balcony, she would smell the fish cooking. It had wafted in sometimes through the front door as well.

"Mr Anirban Dasgupta does not want to eat fish now," said Harinmoy.

"Really? How is that possible?" Reena put down her teacup.

"You see, when *seedhi ungli se ghee nahi nikalta hai...* then you have to use crooked means."

"Yes, so?"

"I hatched a plan. You see, Sharmila... oh, what a name, beautiful is it not, dear?"

Was Harinmoy half in love with Sharmila himself?

"You are fond of Sharmila?" Reena raised her eyebrow.

"No, Reenaji, I love the name, not the lady. She was creating problem in the marriage, *na*?"

"Well, Mr Dasgupta brought her here. He is responsible, and his love for fish is responsible." Reena laid it out, cut and dried and salted.

"A matter of perspective, Madam, it is always a matter of perspective. Coming back to fish, you see, Sharmila cooked the fish. So many recipes Madam, fish in mustard sauce, steamed fish, fish with *brinjal*, smoked fish, fish cutlets... my mouth waters thinking of it."

Reena carefully removed a hair strand from where it had ensnared itself in the frame of her spectacles. Then she carefully placed her spectacles on the table.

She said, "I am being very patient, Harinmoy. Please tell me what happened, you are becoming too fond of the fish in the whole story. I know fish dishes."

"I love fish too, Madam, but I had to help Prateeksha, is it not, dear? She was the one whose interests were weighing on my mind all the time."

"Yes, yes." Reena did not want to know about fish, she wanted to know how there was no more fish.

"*Na rehega bans, na bajegi bansuri, Reenaji.* I had to remove the source of it all; not the lovely cook, not the delicious fish, but Anirban's undesirable craving for fish in mouth."

"*Fish in mouth*? Sounds like a disease. So what did you do?"

"I found a way out, a mantra. I whispered it in Prateeksha's ear."

"And...?" Reena leaned forward. The need to know was driving her crazy.

Reena pushed the bowls of roasted peanuts and diet *chiwda*, already placed by her earlier on the table, towards him. "Harinmoy, these are oil-free, please have some," she said.

"Oil-free, Madam? That is nothing. I will tell you the formula I devised for fish-free. Everything needs a formula."

His mobile rang. "Oh, yes, coming..." he said into the phone.

He looked at Reena, his eyes apologetic. "Have to go, urgent work, sorry for the disturbance, will come again and talk."

"Harinmoy, you can't leave like this! You must tell me what you did."

"Madam, I will. But I cannot tell you in a jiffy. And I have to leave in a jiffy."

Reena watched him pick up his jacket, goggles and hat and head out towards the door. She stood up to see him out. As she walked to the front door, she eyed the roasted peanuts on the table, and clasping her hands behind her back, forced herself not to reach for a handful.

Dish without Fish

"Madam Reenaji, how are you?" A few days later, Harinmoy had returned, looking as pleased as a pickle, his grin stretching from ear to ear.

"Madam Reenaji, I had said I would tell you the formula for being a Super Sleuth like me, but I could not do so. However, now I can tell you what happened in the Dasgupta household, Flat No. 69, after I whispered the mantra in Prateeksha's ear."

Reena removed the plugs from her ears. She had been listening to a TED talk. "Hello, Harinmoy, I am all ears," she smiled.

The tubby man sat down, breathed in, then breathed out. "What a triumph," he said, "Madam, you must put some extra cardamom in the tea..."

Reena brought the tea out and they sat at the dining table, facing each other, smiling. "So tell me, Harinmoy," said Reena, "I have waited some time for this."

Harinmoy spoke. "Madam, this has been told to me by Prateeksha herself.

"Sharmila used to cook the fish but Anirban always wanted Prateeksha to serve the food, and then sit next to him while he ate. Prateeksha forced herself to serve the fish, though she hated its smell. It was a reluctant act.

"So the first time after I whispered the magic formula in her ear, Prateeksha brought the fish to him and also wore a Dakhai cotton *sari* as she served the food. She looked particularly beautiful to Anirban in the *sari*, and smiled when he complimented her.

"She had sent Sharmila to fetch something so that she could serve the fish. Before bringing the dish from the kitchen, she sprinkled a whole lot of salt on the fish. She mixed it in well before serving the fish curry to Anirban.

"Anirban could not eat his FISH...

"He screamed at Sharmila, who had returned to the kitchen by then. Sharmila started crying. He was penitent, and asked for forgiveness. After all, she was his cook, the one who made fish the way he liked it. He could not lose her.

"The next day, Prateeksha sent Sharmila to the vegetable seller below to fetch some green chillies. Meanwhile, she put lots of raw mustard oil, in the already cooked dish, which she then served to Anirban. Anirban just got up from the table and left in anger.

"Not for once did the man try to figure out what was suddenly going wrong. All he knew was he was not getting fish to eat. He felt starved and deprived.

"The third day, Prateeksha quietly took the fish from the fridge at night and left it outside. In the early morning, she sneaked it back in. The whole place reeked of fish in the morning. Moreover, the fish had rotted... it could not be cooked.

"Anirban screamed at Sharmila and asked her to leave. '*Tumi jao, jao.*'

"Sharmila had tears in her eyes. She said, '*Aami jaachchi.*' She went to her room to gather her *saris*.

"Prateeksha was puking on the fourth morning. She felt so sick with the smell of fish and the fact that she had handled it up close for the last three days.

"Anirban thought she was puking for other reasons and he put a gentle arm around her. 'Do you want to go to the doctor?' he asked her.

"Prateeksha played it smart and said, 'Let's wait and watch.' She played it even smarter and said that in her *delicate* condition, she could not bear to smell fish around.

"Anirban had already begun to have second thoughts about the fish being cooked. In three days, his taste buds had undergone a change. He told Prateeksha that he would give up fish altogether, or at least till... their child was born.

"Prateeksha could not let it go at that. She made him promise that the child would be brought up as a vegetarian."

Harinmoy leaned back and looked at Reena, his face wreathed with smiles. "Anirban wanted to rush her once again to the doctor but Prateeksha told him that they should wait and see.

"But she also told me later that Anirban has been grinning from ear to ear, despite the loss of fish. He seems to be so sure that he will become a father.

"What a victory, Madam! My plan has worked wonders."

~

"Suppose she isn't pregnant?" Reena asked, sipping her tea.

"Madam, you and I know she is not. She was puking because of the fish."

"So Anirban will know eventually."

"Not really. We also know that she can soon be."

"Wha-at?" The thought had often crossed Reena's mind that Harinmoy talked the most ridiculous things to her and got away with them too.

"Prateeksha may not have had plans to have a child, but she is smart. She knows that if she bears a child now, Anirban will give up fish altogether. He may give up non-vegetarian food to have her happy in the kitchen. The smell of cauliflower fritters and not chicken fry will assail your nostrils then, is it not, dear?" He grinned some more, the dimple in his left cheek dancing.

"So, other plans are afoot," Reena said, sipping her tea. Well, at least Prateeksha would no longer sob on Anand's shoulder. That was a relief. She sighed, thinking of how she had doubts about Prateeksha and Prateeksha had doubts about Sharmila, and so on.

"What happened to Sharmila?" she asked.

"She left. Her days in Delhi were over. Without the fish, there was no use for her. Prateeksha gave her many *saris* which she did not want, a silver ring and some pearl earrings and said she should never show her face here again."

"Bribed her?"

"All fair in love and war and dish without fish."

"Oh, yes!" said Reena.

◆ 30 ◆

White Shoes with Brass Buckles

Harinmoy had come to say goodbye to Reena. He had an international case to investigate and planned to leave for Bangkok soon. Reena set aside the jewellery design she was working on for a client in Bangalore, a young professional who wanted two sets, one for everyday office wear and another to wear to office parties.

Harinmoy sighed. He said, "You know, Reenaji, when I first came to Delhi, I was new to the place and did not know my way about. Delhi is only for smart people, it does not suffer fools gladly. I have learnt this the hard way.

"See, one incident I will tell you. I had just moved to Delhi and taken a job recently.

"I wanted to go from Bhajanpura where I was staying at that time, to Azadpur, to meet a friend. I did not have much money with me. I climbed onto a DTC bus and told the ticket conductor where I wanted to go. He cut me a Rupee 6/- ticket and gave me the change, which I put in my pocket. I took the ticket and also placed it in my pocket.

"At Model Town, the TT came, had one look at my ticket, and forced me to get off the bus. It seems I had not paid the required fare for where I had to go.

"I was a bit dazed by this. 'I paid what the conductor had asked me to pay,' I told the TT. But the TT said I should have paid more and so he fined me Rupees 20/-. Now I did not have that amount in my pocket. I only had Rupees 12/-, which he took. I did not know how to pay him the balance amount.

"So I said to him, 'Here are my shoes. Keep them, I will arrange the money and then take them back.'

"They were not expensive like these I am wearing now, but they were the only pair I had," he said. Harinmoy looked at his white pointed shoes and Reena smiled wide, to stop herself from grimacing. These, expensive? She would not pick them up if they came along free and with a gift thrown in.

Harinmoy continued, "So I left the shoes behind, and the TT kept them at the *paan-waala's,* whose shop was close to where we were standing. He told that thin, sticky, betel-leaf shop owner to take care of my shoes!

"Now I am a *manjha hua khilaadi* as you say, Reena Madam," he said, "a seasonal player."

"Not seasonal," Reena interjected, "seasoned."

"Same same, that only, I mean."

He closed his eyes, leaned back, gave a deep sigh, and opened his eyes again.

"But then I was new, I am talking of seven years back, Madam. I walked barefoot to my friend's house and luckily I was slim those days, fresh from my own village and also knew the way to my friend, Sunil's house, since I had been there a couple of times.

"The landlord saw me walk in barefoot and stared, 'Hello, Harinmoy, you know you are not wearing your shoes today?' Trust him to notice. But despite my frustration and burning feet, for I had been walking in the sun and the pavement was hot, I smiled and said, 'Sir, today is my fast, and I do not wear shoes today as part of the *puja.*' The landlord nodded happily at my answer and did not wonder at it at all, because *puja* is something everyone accepts, it calls for all kinds of weird sacrifices.

"I went to my friend's room on the first floor and told him what had happened. He caught hold of a policeman who was a neighbour and a friend, and who was off-duty that day, luckily for me, and we rode on my friend's scooter, the three of us... to the *paan-waala's* shop.

"I got off the scooter and saw that the TT was busy apprehending some more bus travellers. Maybe he had some understanding with the bus conductor, you know. Like give the unsuspecting new traveller a wrong ticket and then make him pay through his nose to the TT. And then they would split the profits?"

He looked expectantly at Reena. "Lovely day today, is it not dear?"

Reena said, "Yes, but it's kind of sad that you are leaving. Let's have some tea."

She returned with two cups, and placed his blue one, with the yellow flowers, next to him. Hers was orange, with a black horse on it. It was her Black Beauty cup, the one she brought out on special occasions, when she needed some extra comfort.

He looked at her cup and said, "Ah! New cup, Madam?"

"No, I just use it sometimes."

"Well, I galloped like this black horse on your cup. The TT was a distance from the *paan* shop and I quickly bent down, picked up my shoes and ran. I jumped on to the scooter and we were off.

"The *paan-waala* in the meantime had realized what had happened and he shouted at the TT, *'jootey le gaya. Le gaya!'*

"The TT heard him and began running after our scooter. I grinned merrily and waved my shoes in the air as bait for him, the bastard. Sorry Madam, forgive, sometimes I have to swear."

Reena kept a straight face. Too much rope was not to be given, even to friendly, well-meaning sleuths.

He continued, "Best of all, as I saw him running after us, I also saw that the people he had apprehended had taken off while he chased after my shoes. Served him right."

He looked down and studied his shoes seriously. "Maybe that is why I am so attached to my shoes now, having had the experience of losing them."

Reena looked at the white, shining, pointed, unblinking shoes, with their wide brass buckles. "You've earned them," she said.

◆ 31 ◆

Unforgettable Due to Formula

Reena finally mustered up her courage to ask Harinmoy before he left for Thailand and his new project, "Why do you wear such colourful clothes?"

Harinmoy had come to say his final goodbye, and had brought her a farewell gift. She had not opened the package yet.

"Madam, a cup of tea, please. This is a formula, you know."

Another formula? Reena was foxed. "Sure, tea coming up," she said.

Harinmoy looked at the blue teacup in which Reena served him the tea. He said, "Reenaji, I will never forget this cup. Or you, for that matter."

"Why should you forget me? No need to, when you can always drop in any time," Reena said. Her words were sincere, for she had become very fond of the man. She felt comfortable in his company, and he had helped her understand many things, one major one being that you should never judge a book by its cover, or a man by his dress-sense.

He brushed his hair off his face with a smile. "Yes, of course, after all, I would also need your help at times, Madam SS."

"Well, after RR, SS is the only way forward," she said.

"Joking again, is it not, dear?" he said. "Yes, I also dress the way I do to make a forward statement."

"Really?" said Reena. "What do you mean?"

"See," he said, "I told you about when I arrived in Delhi, seven years ago, from my village. I took a job. I was short, thin, dressed in ordinary T-shirt and grey pants, and would not get a second glance. I was a nobody.

"But I did not want to remain a nobody. I had to devise a formula for myself. How to get where I want to be. It was a chance talk with a friend that led me to think, why not be a private investigator? I have always been interested in people and their lives.

"I am intuitive, I can sense things. Then, I have good deductive powers, I am observant. For example, how many people will notice the fact that whenever Prateeksha walks into your house, your colour changes?"

"Oh... it's not so bad..." said Reena, turning red in the face.

"Madam, your husband has eyes only for you. But you cannot see that because he is a charming man, and what is natural for him, becomes a source of suspicion for you."

"Uh..." said Reena, suddenly focusing hard on pushing a wayward hair strand behind her ear. "I give him a lot of rope... I am not possessive."

"Yet you wonder at his fondness for a young, smart woman like Prateeksha. Mr Anand has the dangerous charm; I think perhaps your son has it too? They cannot help the attraction they hold for other women. But you have to understand that you are the Universe for him. Long time I have been wanting to tell you this, now it is out."

"Oh," said Reena, pulling her *dupatta* around her shoulders and looking away from him.

She was flustered and rather taken aback by Harinmoy's talk. If she had not known Harinmoy for what he was, she would have thought that Anand had primed him. She began to smile at the thought of both of them together, hatching the plan to make sure she saw the truth of Anand's love for her.

"And your face lights up when you smile, Madam," he said. "Mr Anand is a lucky man."

"Oh, Harinmoy, thank you! I don't know what to say."

"Nothing to say, Madam, only to understand."

~

"Okay," said Reena, "please continue with your formula story. You stopped it mid-way."

"Coming back to my story, Madam, I decided to become an investigator. So I got my visiting cards made, sent out flyers and rented an office.

"But people had to remember me, I had to stand out. I needed a formula for this. I thought, people always remember heroes, and each hero has a certain style, a certain way of dressing, a certain voice. I worked on my voice, made it deeper. Such a voice is more dependable.

"I also needed a makeover. I have worshipped Jeetendra, Dev Anand and Rajnikant as my heroes. So I picked up their dress code and style. Dev Anand wore vibrant colours. I do too."

Reena took in his orange shirt and green pants and sighed. A bright yellow handkerchief hung out of his pocket.

"Jeetendra wore sober clothes, but his white shoes stood out. So I wear them."

Reena kept her gaze on his face, and did not look at his patent leather shoes.

"Rajnikant wore goggles and a cowboy hat, I wear these too. I think I am picture perfect."

Reena could not help herself. "A hero? Why didn't you join films?"

"Hero, yes?" He smiled. "In my own line, is it not, dear? I wanted to be successful fast, assuredly so. My field did not have many aspirants. There was a gap which needed to be filled with my expertise. So, here I am, at your doorstep."

"In my dining room, actually," Reena laughed. "A really unforgettable persona..."

"Thank you, Madam, everything works with formula."

Reena picked up the gift from where she had placed it on the table. She carefully prised off the tape and removed the brown paper wrapping. She held it up to the light streaming in through the windows. It was a small statue of a fisherwoman painted in garish pink and blue, with plump red lips, and a basket of fish on her head. The scales of the tiny fish gleamed silver.

She was quite overcome. "It's lovely," she said. "Thank you."

"Something to remind you of our first work together, Madam SS."

"So I will write, RR, Jewellery Designer, SS, on my visiting cards?"

"You will surely fox them all, Madam. It is a formula, is it not, dear?" He raised his hand and they high-fived across the table.

◆ 32 ◆

Crowning Glory

Reena sat in the cane chair on the balcony, combing her hair. She saw Anand watching her.

"Any grey showing?" she asked.

"No, none," he was quick to reassure her, knowing how conscious she was of even a little grey.

She put the comb down and lifted her hair off her neck. It was still thick and heavy though it was not as long as it used to be. Now she trimmed it to shoulder length. It made it manageable.

"You know," she said, "when I was using that famous brand 'Lustre', to colour my hair, so expensive... but it gave such glints..."

Anand waited, knowing her eagerness to talk about her hair.

"Well, though it gave a good colour and highlights, I lost a lot of hair, even started balding from the front a bit..."

"All these things have chemicals in them," Anand admonished. As if she would listen, he thought to himself. Her one *real* vanity was her crowning glory.

"I know, but it was only when my skin began to get so sensitive, that I gave up colour and perfumes. But to go without hair colour was so tough."

"I know," he sympathized.

"So I tried all kinds of things, henna which just turned the grey a bright orange, as though I was one of the Haj-returned worshippers.

"Then I tried 'Black Henna Powder' from the Khadi GramUdyog which is supposed to have no colouring matter other than natural, which made my grey hair purple.

"Remember Minna asking me if I had coloured my hair pink, this was when the colour was fading, and I told her no, I had coloured it purple and that stumped her. But then she asked why you had not followed suit."

Anand grinned. He had been told his salt and pepper look gave him a distinguished air. And he was not balding yet.

She continued, "Well, actually the fact is that I have now begun to use this much cheaper Indian hair colour, that only colours the hair black, but what do I care, I want black, not grey. My hair has stopped shedding since I stopped using 'Lustre'. I am so happy.

"Moreover, see this," she said, pointing to the right side of her scalp, where a little curl peeped from under the rest of her hair. "This is hair growing back in the bald spot!" She smiled.

He said, "That is what we do every night. The kids and I are replacing the lost hair, strand by strand, in the night."

She laughed. "You are funny. And, how come I don't know this?" she shot back, arching an eyebrow.

"Oh," he said, not the hint of a smile on his face, "you are a good horse trader, that's why..."

Reena knew she slept like a log. She never heard anything once her head hit the pillow.

"Well, at least I bring in the profits," she smiled.

"And we are paying you back with hair," he grinned now.

She began to giggle like a young girl and Anand said, "That's what I love to see, the mirth in your eyes and the smile on your face. A rather rare phenomenon nowadays."

• Epilogue •

The Fish Arrives

Prateeksha and her husband, Anirban Dasgupta, were finally fishless and happy.

Harinmoy was away in Bangkok. He was there to solve a case and he was also very happy. He would charge the same rate, but in Bhats, so he would earn more than double of what he earned in India.

Reena was happy, for Anand was no longer required to give his shoulder for Prateeksha to sob on. In fact, Reena had become friends with Prateeksha, as Prateeksha turned more and more towards Reena for advice regarding the baby she was expecting.

~

One fine Sunday morning, Reena was with Prateeksha in her flat. Prateeksha had called Reena over to learn how to make *aloo-paranthas* the right way, the Reena Rajan way.

The doorbell rang and Prateeksha walked carefully to the door to open it. She then ran back into the arms of Anirban, pointing to the open doorway and crying, "Fish, fish."

He went out, had a look at the fat fish lying on his doormat, and, despite its state, fell in love with fish again.

"*Aami maach khabo*," he whispered. Prateeksha heard him and began to cry louder.

Reena saw all that was happening and decided to take charge. She picked up her mobile and called Harinmoy. He answered the phone immediately.

"Harinmoy," she said, "come quick. There is fish in the neighbourhood again. We just have too many fish to fry here!"

Harinmoy replied, "Madam, how nice of you to call. But you know I am in Bangkok. I have seaweed and shrimp here. I will come with it soon." He paused. "You are of course joking, Madam, there is no fish around now?"

"No, no, there is fish right here, as in real fish... as in things are fishy, Harinmoy. Prateeksha's crying."

"Okay. O-kay. Will sew things here tight and then catch a flight. Coming soon to you, is it not, dear?"

~

Reena held on to a sobbing Prateeksha in the drawing room of Flat No. 69, while Anirban in the bedroom, called the fishmonger. "*Aekta Ilish maach. Aekhoni.* At once. Bring to Flat No. 69 of Mr Anirban Dasgupto."

Prateeksha sobbed, "Reena Auntie, I am coming to your house to stay. My child cannot be born among rotten, smelly things." She placed her hand on her stomach, looked at it and said, "Don't you worry, *you* will grow up a good vegetarian."

"Over my dead body," said Anirban, coming out of the bedroom. "He is a Bengali child. He will eat Bengali food. I will teach him how to take out the bones from the fish carefully. I will make him appreciate the value of fish. Fish is good for the brain, you know that, Proteeksha!"

"Yes, yes, she is wearing spectacles inside here, reading Tagore in the womb itself, this Bengali baby!" Prateeksha sobbed louder.

"*Arre*, all the time crying, Proteeksha, the baby will be born crying..." Anirban's face was red with anger.

"All your fault," she said, "forcing fish down our throats."

"*Arre*, you both, stop it, all babies are born crying," said Reena. She looked at the fish that lay innocently at the door. "Anirban, please remove this. I have to go to my flat now."

"I will remove it only on one condition. You will go. She..." he looked at Prateeksha, "... will not follow you."

Prateeksha ran crying into the bedroom as Anirban took a bag and stepped towards the fish to pick it up. It had begun to smell but this did not seem to bother him. He picked it up, put it in the bag, and said, "Just going to put it in the garbage bin outside, Reenaji, please stay with Proteeksha..."

Reena sat down. Just when everything was going well, trouble had arrived once more at the door.

She wondered who was responsible. Perhaps it was Sharmila, the scorned woman, getting back at them? Perhaps it was just the jinx of Flat No. 69 playing itself out?

It would take the Super Sleuth combo to figure it out.

Is it not, dear?

Glossary of Terms

Aami jaachchi: I am going. (Bengali)
Aami maach khabo: I will eat fish. (Bengali)
Aap kaun?: Who are you?
Aekhoni: At once. (Bengali)
Aekta: One. (Bengali)
Aloo-paranthas: Indian flatbread made of wheat flour and stuffed with spiced, boiled mashed potatoes.
Arre: Used as a general term, to show surprise, shock.
Bakra: Goat, also used to denote sacrificial goat / victim.
Behenji: Sister. Used also as a general form of address to show respect.
Beti: Daughter. In India, this term is used in general, when an elder addresses a young girl, who may not be related in any way.
Bhaiya: Brother. Used also as a general form of address to show respect.
Brinjal: Eggplant or aubergine.
Chai-waala: Roadside tea-stall owner.
Chikna: Glossy, smooth.
Chiwda: Snack of rice flakes.
Chulah: A brick oven filled with charcoal, a traditional Indian stove for cooking.
Churidars: Tight, leg-hugging, cotton pants worn by both men and women. These are wrinkled from the calf to the ankle.
Daane daane pe likha hai khane wale ka naam: On each morsel is written the name of the person destined to eat it.

Dhaba: Roadside restaurants usually situated on highways, serving cheap, hot, simple local cuisine.
Dhobi: Man who washes and irons clothes.
Dholak: Two-headed hand drum.
Dilli ka jhatka: A dance step from Delhi.
Diwali / Deepawali: The Festival of Lights is the biggest Indian festival celebrated all over India in October or November. The festival celebrates the victory of light over darkness and good over evil. On Diwali night, prayers are offered to Lakshmi, the goddess of wealth and prosperity. Homes are lit with earthen lamps and candles, fireworks light up the sky, and families and friends celebrate with food and sweets.
Dupatta: A 2.5 metre long piece of chiffon / cotton / other fine material cloth draped over the breasts and over both shoulders, with the end pieces hanging at the back on both sides.
Ghagra-cholis: short blouses and long, flowing skirts.
Ghagra-kameez: A traditional Indian dress.
Gujiya: A classic Indian sweet dumpling considered among Holi festival's special dishes.
Gulabjamun: Deep fried, dark coloured, sweet dumplings, stewed in sugar syrup.
Gutti: A rawl plug chiseled out of wood.
Haan: Yes. (Hindi)
Hain: Yes. (Bengali)
Hilsa: A type of fish.
Ho gaya: (It) is done.
Holi: A Spring festival of colours, celebrated by Indians, usually in March.
Humey pata hai ji: We know.
Ilish maach: Hilsa fish, very popular with Bengalis.
Istri-waala: Man who irons clothes.
Ji: General term used to show respect.
Jootey le gaya: Taken the shoes.
Jugaadpan: The ability to find workable solutions.

Kameez: A long shirt-like dress with slit sides, worn over a *salwar / churidaar*.
Kaun hai?: Who is there?
Khoya: Prepared by thickening milk to 1/5 its consistency, and used as a base for a wide variety of Indian sweets.
Kripa: Benevolence.
Kurta: A loose, long shirt-like dress which can be worn by both men and women over a *salwar* or *churidaar*.
Kya lengii aap?: What will you have?
Lehenga: A long, flared skirt.
Manjha hua khilaadi: One who knows the ropes.
Memsahib: Used to address a lady. A throwback from the British colonial days.
Mohallas: Neighbourhoods.
Motichoor laddoo: Standard Indian sweet served for any celebration.
Motichoor kesar laddoo: Standard Indian sweet with the flavour of saffron added to it.
Na?: Used at the end of a sentence, it denotes a question like 'isn't it'? Also denotes no, when used otherwise.
Nahin: No.
Namaste: Greeting.
Na rehega bans, na bajegi bansuri: If there is no bamboo, there will be no flute. (If the source of trouble is removed, then the trouble won't occur.)
Paani: Water.
Paan-waala: Shopkeeper selling betel leaves.
Pakodas: Fritters made of gram flour.
Pallu: The end of the sari.
Poha: A light breakfast dish made of flattened rice.
Pranayam: Yogic breath-control exercises.
Pucca: Absolute, firm.
Puja: Prayer/s. There are many types of, and occasions for Puja, which can be performed individually and privately; or collectively as a religious function.

Rosogulla / Rasgulla: a cheese-based, syrupy dessert popular in the Indian subcontinent, particularly in the Indian states of Odisha and West Bengal.

Rotis: Unleavened bread made from wholewheat flour.

Sahib: Used to address a gentleman. A throwback from the British colonial days.

Salaam: A form of greeting.

Salwar: This forms the lower part of a traditional Indian dress, and is worn with a kurta on top. Traditionally an outfit of the Punjab (*salwar-kurta*), it is now commonly worn by most Indian women for comfortable movement.

Sangeet: A song ceremony before the marriage when family and friends gather to sing rather bawdy and naughty songs. It is more of a ladies' event, though now some men also join in.

Sari: Traditional Indian wear for women consisting of a 5.5 metre of cloth draped around the body. The sari is worn over a petticoat. The woman also wears a short blouse to match the sari.

Seedhi ungli se ghee nahi nikalta hai: You cannot take out clarified butter with a straight finger. (You have to use crooked means where straight ones won't work.)

Shanti: Peace.

Sherwanis: Traditional tunic worn by men.

Supari: Betel nut.

Sutra: The root or thread that holds everything together.

Tandoori rotis: Unleavened bread made from wholewheat flour, cooked in a clay oven.

Thikana: Address.

Total ho gai si: Totally wrecked. (Punjabi)

Tumi jao: You go. (Bengali)

Wah: Great!

Zari: Even thread traditionally made of fine gold or silver used in traditional Indian, Pakistani and Persian garments, especially as brocade in saris.

Thanks

In gratitude to my mentors, for their unshakable belief in my writing ability.

My deep gratitude to Chris Galvin Nguyen for her Foreword, and also to Susan Tepper, Nandita Bose, Vasudev Murthy, Luisa Brenta and Christopher Allen, who read the manuscript pre-publication, and took the time to write the blurbs.

Thanks to the wonderful Matt Potter who is fully responsible for the writing of this book. He said Pure Slush would publish; I just needed to tell the stories. It is support like this that makes a writer.

A big thank you to my family, who put up with me the way I am, and agree they would have it no other way. But then, I am speaking for them here, and maybe I am colouring this a bit in my favour.

~ Abha Iyengar, New Delhi, September 2014

About the Author

Abha Iyengar is an award winning, internationally published poet, author, essayist and a British Council certified creative writing mentor. She is a member of The Asia-Pacific Writers and Translators Association.

Her work has appeared in Pure Slush, Flash Frontier, The Four Quarters Magazine, Door Knobs and Body Paint, Bewildering Stories and others. She is a Kota Press Poetry Anthology Contest winner. Her story, *The High Stool*, was nominated for the Story South Million Writers Award. Her poem-film, *Parwaaz*, was selected for the Indian Panorama, and won a Special Jury prize in Patras, Greece. Her stories have been selected for A Rainbow Feast: New Asian Short Stories, The Asian Writer, Vaani and The Indo-Australian Anthology of Short Fiction. She has received the Lavanya Sankaran Writing Fellowship for 2009-2010. She also received the Mariner Award 2010. She was Featured Poet at Poetry with Prakriti, 2010. She has been honoured with the BTB Literary Award 2012 for Best Fiction in a New Genre.

Abha's poems have recently appeared in The Anthology of Contemporary Indian Poetry edited by Menka Shivdasani. She was among the top 15 finalists at Flash Mob 2013, an international event.

Her other published works include *Yearnings* (poetry collection), *Flash Bites* (flash fiction), and *Shrayan* (fantasy novel). She dabbles in street photography and digital art. Find her website at *www.abhaiyengar.com*, and her blog at *www.abhaencounter.blogspot.in*

Other books from *Pure Slush*

Visit the *Pure Slush* Store online:
http://pureslush.webs.com/store.htm

 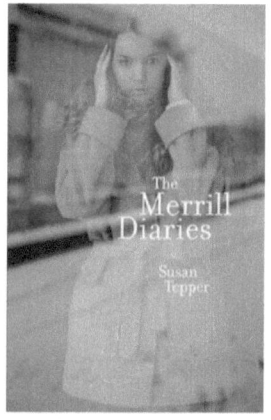

The Company of Men
by Luisa Brenta
ISBN: 978-1-925101-06-5

The Vixen Scream
by Nancy Stohlman
ISBN: 978-1-925101-11-9

The Merrill Diaries
by Susan Tepper
ISBN: 978-0-9922778-2-6

 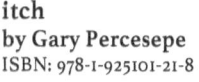  

itch
by Gary Percesepe
ISBN: 978-1-925101-21-8

Hard
by Dusty-Anne Rhodes
ISBN: 978-1-925101-80-5

Glass Animals
by Stephen V. Ramey
ISBN: 978-1-925101-86-7